PLEASE PUT YOUR
BRAND HERE!
Thank You.

EASY MONEY

Center Point
Large Print

Also by Will Cook and available from
Center Point Large Print:

Bandit's Trail
The Breakthrough

**This Large Print Book carries the
Seal of Approval of N.A.V.H.**

EASY MONEY

WILL COOK

CENTER POINT LARGE PRINT
THORNDIKE, MAINE

This Center Point Large Print edition
is published in the year 2022 by arrangement with
Golden West Literary Agency.

Originally published in the US by Perma Books.
Originally published in the UK by Robert Hale.

The text of this Large Print edition is unabridged.
In other aspects, this book may vary
from the original edition.
Printed in the United States of America
on permanent paper sourced using
environmentally responsible foresting methods.
Set in 16-point Times New Roman type.

ISBN: 978-1-63808-257-6 (hardcover)
ISBN: 978-1-63808-261-3 (paperback)

The Library of Congress has cataloged this record
under Library of Congress Control Number: 2021950764

EASY MONEY

Chapter One

In the wild and untamed Wyoming country during the early eighteen-eighties, there was much to try a man's soul. The summer heat was often blistering and the winter cold a force that froze the mind to a dangerous numbness. In this vastness, there were deserts and rich valleys and mountains that lay as a continuous upheaval.

This was her face, and beneath it there was wealth, calling to men who were strong enough to seize and claim it for their own. Men heard this call and answered it, some to build, while others, in their desire to claim, destroyed.

But this moral debate never entered the thoughts of Meade Bigelow, for he had his job and his dreams and they left little time for anything else.

Erected against the sloping face of a towering mountain, another in a straggling chain of mountains, the many buildings of the Great Northern Mining and Smelting Company made dark shadows against the blacker envelopment of the night. In one building, set aside from the others, lamplight made yellow squares in the windows and a man paced back and forth across a room that was low and wide, with a huge desk sitting in the middle of it.

Quite possibly Meade Bigelow's concern had turned to definite anger three months before, when the first of the ore stages was halted and nine thousand in silver stolen. On his desk now was the teamster's latest report—another robbery which had netted a cool ten thousand. Only this time there would be no more guessing. The robber had been identified.

Bigelow moved around the room, a big man with a deep restlessness upon him. Going to the end door, he opened it and spoke softly to the man who worked over the ledgers. "See if you can find Garvey and send him in to me."

The man nodded and vacated his stool. Meade closed the door, then sat on the corner of his desk, puffing deeply on his cigar. He was a large man, heavy in the shoulders and arms, and on his square-cut face there was a certain primitiveness, as though his Maker had been in a hurry and had left the job before the rough edges were smoothed out.

His hair was light, almost blond; his eyes were a pale gray. He wore his hair long over the ears, touching his collar in back in a waterfall haircut. In spite of the trend toward side whiskers and a short beard, Meade Bigelow confined his mustache to a clipped fullness that filled his heavy upper lip. He wore black trousers, the bottom half of an expensive suit, but the cuffs were stuffed into mule-ear boots with a trace of mud around the sole and heel. The white linen shirt he wore stood out sharply against the darkness of his skin, and a black tie was carelessly knotted; one end dangled an inch below the other.

Twice he removed his hunting-case watch and popped the lids before time reduced his cigar to a sour stub. Then the door opened and a rough-looking man came in, a holstered revolver slapping against his thigh.

Plucking the report from his desk, Meade Bigelow said, "Are you sure this is right, Garvey?"

The man shifted his feet and remembered to remove his sweat-stained hat. "I seen him, just like I said. There was enough moon to see by. The other two was in the brush, but I seen him as plain as I can see you."

"A man might get killed over this," Bigelow said flatly. "There is no room here for a mistake."

"Jesus Christ!" Garvey said. "I told you—what more do you want?"

"All right," Bigelow said and tossed the report on his desk. "You can go, Garvey."

The man nodded and shuffled out, closing the door behind him. Bigelow moved across the room to a wall closet, got his coat and tossed it on the desk. From the middle drawer, he took a shoulder holster and spent a minute adjusting it under his left armpit. The elastic cord ran across his back, hooked beneath the right armpit; the bottom was secured by passing his belt through a leather loop. From the same drawer he lifted his gun, a short-barreled Frontier Colt. He spread the spring and settled the gun in place, and then opened a box of cartridges, dumping a handful of blunt-nosed .44-40's into his pocket.

Shrugging into his coat, Bigelow blew out the lamp. He went out, and as he closed the door, paused to read the sign, metal letters fastened to the mahogany:

MEADE BIGELOW
General Superintendent
Great Northern Mining and Smelting Company

A small smile lifted the ends of his lips, and he touched the chief clerk lightly on the shoulder in passing. "Good night, Cord."

"Good night, Mr. Bigelow."

Bigelow paused on the building steps to look out over the land. Three miles away, and four thousand feet below on the valley floor, Silver City sparkled with the glow of many lights.

He extracted another cigar from his pocket and fired it. From the shadows of an adjoining building a tall man detached himself, and Bigelow said, "Saddle my horse, Clymer."

The man moved away, and Bigelow sat down on the steps to wait. He liked it here, where he could see for miles and listen and hear no sounds.

The mines were closed at night, and there was nothing but the muted movement of guards to interrupt the quiet.

To Meade Bigelow, this sense of peace was worth the effort spent in building his success. The years of study and field work were behind him, and at thirty-four, he could look back on his life and know that he had done well with himself.

The practical side of his mind told him different. Great Northern was being robbed, and while that happened, he was not doing his job.

Clymer came up with the horse, and Bigelow stepped into the saddle. He turned immediately down the trail leading to Silver City. Because he was a mild-mannered man, Meade did not like to form an opinion so definite that altering it at a later date would be difficult, but the evidence now was too strong to ignore. Yet there was a contrary streak in Bigelow. He displayed it by riding instead of driving a buggy behind a pair of matched bays, by refusing to wear fine suits and a plug hat. All this pointed to his independence.

An hour's easy ride carried him to the end of Lode Street, and he dismounted in front of Allendale's Bank, where a light made a yellow sliver beneath the drawn shade. He crossed the boardwalk, rapped lightly on the door, then heard Fred Allendale's answering footsteps.

"Who is it?" Allendale asked.

"Meade."

The bolt slid back, and the door opened. Meade stepped in and waited for Allendale to lock it again, then followed the slim man to the back office.

Allendale's tastes ran to money and books. He waved Bigelow into an overstuffed leather chair and offered a cigar, which Meade accepted. "Did you find out anything?" Allendale asked.

"Garvey swears he saw him," Meade said. "I'll go on that."

The banker closed the book he had been reading and studied Bigelow. "You're angry now, Meade. Wait until you cool off."

"A man was killed," Bigelow said softly.

"I heard about it," Allendale said. "The whole town knows." He leaned forward in his chair. "Let Jim Hardesty handle it, Meade. He's the law."

Meade shifted his heavy-boned frame in the chair and stretched his legs, a man troubled and trying not to show it. To Allendale, who watched men carefully and read them, this was enough to cause worry. Bigelow raised a hand and scrubbed his face. He said, "Has Murray Sinclair or his brothers—No, they wouldn't be that stupid."

"They haul their ore to Denver," Allendale said. "Meade, let this thing ride for a day or two. Something might turn up."

"Can't," Meade murmured and stood up. He cuffed his hat against his leg a few times, then added, "I'm putting up at the hotel. They have to come into town sometime, and I'll be here."

"I'd let Hardesty handle it," Allendale repeated, but Meade turned to the door. "Murray might have an alibi—have you thought of that?"

"Do you think so?" Bigelow shook his head. "We'll see when he comes in town."

Fred Allendale gnawed his lip, not knowing what to say. He was a careful man in a careful business where an error in judgment could throw him into bankruptcy. For all his careful gauging, he could find no exact clue to Meade Bigelow's disposition.

"It's mighty easy for a man to make a mistake," Allendale cautioned. "Especially a man in your position. I'd be damned sure before I did anything."

"I'll be sure," Meade said and put on his hat before going out.

Across the street Amy Falcon's Restaurant was open, and this reminded him that he had skipped his supper. For a moment he considered crossing the street. Then he remembered other business and turned north, walking until he came to a side street.

Darkness was thick here, and he moved slowly, turning again on a back street where the residential section stood away from the road. At a large house, he turned up the path and mounted

13

the porch. He knocked and waited, and then the door opened.

A colored woman smiled and said, "Come right in, Mr. Bigelow. Miss June's upstairs." She took Meade's hat and hurried up the stairs.

From the library to one side of the hall, paper rustled, and Dan Conover came out, smiling and offering his hand. "Good to see you, Meade. Come in."

He was a little man, gray at the temples, but his eyebrows and beard were as black as the night. He had a deep voice, a surprising thing in a body so small, but size did not dim his commanding air or the power he exercised.

Bigelow took a deep chair and accepted an offer of brandy. Cloth rustled on the stairs, and June came in; he put his drink aside and took her hands.

"I can see that I'm in an awkward position here," Conover said and slapped Meade on the shoulder before leaving. His footsteps faded to another part of the house, and June came against Meade, her lips raised for his kiss.

"Darling," she said, "it's been a week."

"A very busy one," he said and kissed her again. She was nearly ten years younger than Bigelow, a small girl, shapely, with an oval face. Her hair was a rich brown, a shade that matched her eyes, and her lips were full, usually composed and not given to easy smiling.

He patted her arm and moved away from her to lift his brandy. She watched him for a moment, briefly irritated at his methodical manner. She pushed this feeling down quickly, for that was the trait that had first attracted her to this man.

Lazy in his motion and speech, Meade was slow to anger and, she remembered with some frustration, slow to take the initiative and kiss her. She had purposely goaded him, and after the kiss he had said, "Well!" as though surprised it had been so painless.

After that he had been sure of himself and kissed her often.

"I heard about the robbery," June said softly. "Meade, was it really Murray?"

He shrugged. "Garvey said that he saw him. Sam and Reilly were with Murray. I want to talk to Murray first."

"And afterward, if he's the one?"

"I think I will just shoot him and have done with it," he said.

"The talk is too serious for me," she said and put her arms around him. "Will you stay for supper?"

"No," he said. "Some other time, June."

She tightened her arms. "Don't go, Meade. I'm a jealous woman, and your job keeps you away too much."

"I'll be back," he said and kissed her again.

The colored woman let him out, and he walked

back to Lode Street and angled across the inter-section toward Karen's Saloon. The building was wide and false-fronted, and Meade pushed the door aside and entered. Bellied against the bar, he ordered a beer, then nursed it along.

Lonigan, who tended bar, said, "Heard about it, Meade. Goofy used to buy his drinks in here."

"Seen Hardesty tonight?" Meade asked.

"Once or twice," Lonigan murmured. "I think he's at Bloom's, getting his hair cut."

"Thanks," Meade said and drained the beer.

He crossed the street again, then walked a half block south to the barbershop. The marshal was the only one there besides Bloom, who held up two mirrors for Hardesty's inspection.

"That's fine," Hardesty said and glanced at the door as Meade paused there, filling it. "How are you, Meade?"

"Unhappy," Meade admitted and studied Hardesty. The man was on the edge of forty and straight as a new rope. A drooping mustache covered his upper lip, half hiding his mouth. He whipped the towel off and stood up. Around his waist, a shell belt drooped, and on his right hip, a pearl-handled Remington dangled from a swivel.

"Let's go to the office," Hardesty suggested and tossed Bloom a quarter.

Traffic on the street was light, and they entered a side lane where the jail sat against the boardwalk. Hardesty inserted his key, then opened the door and went ahead to light a lamp.

Hardesty said, "You're just looking for a great big fight, aren't you, Meade?"

"I'm looking for nearly twenty thousand dollars in silver."

The marshal shook his head. "Murray and his brothers are a pain to you, Meade. After all the others sold out, they stuck it out. You sure there's nothing personal connected with this?"

"Talk plain," Meade suggested.

Hardesty sat down behind his desk and rolled a smoke. "Look at it this way, Meade. Great Northern is the king. All the small claims have been gobbled up, forced to sell out. But Murray Sinclair never did and never will." Hardesty waved his hand at the town. "Look at Silver City, Meade. Is this a boom town where money is to be made?" He shook his head. "A haircut costs twenty-five cents, Meade. I can remember in Alder Gulch when it cost three dollars in dust."

"I don't want to argue economics with you," Meade said. "Controlled wage and organized industry against the get-rich-quick is not the arguing point now. Robbery is the point—and a murder."

Hardesty sighed and slapped the desk. "All right, Meade, I won't argue with you. Up there on the hill you rub elbows with the big augurs, and I guess you're all for the company. But here in Silver City, be careful what you do, Meade. Take that any way you want to."

"All right," Bigelow said. "But get this, Jim. If I think Murray is guilty, you'd better arrest him in a hurry before I get to him. Because if you don't—I'll shoot him."

"That's one way for Great Northern to get his mine," Hardesty said and stared at the closed door after Meade Bigelow went out and down the street.

Amy Falcon's Restaurant was vacant when he went in and took a place at the counter. She came from the kitchen, smiling when she saw him. "The bear has come down from the mountain," she said and leaned on the counter, her arms crossed.

She was taller than most women, and her hair was blonde and sun-bleached. Her eyes were a pale blue, with splinters of laughter in them. She had a full figure, wide-hipped, with ample breasts that pushed against the bodice of her calico dress.

He did not realize that he was staring until she said, "Do I pass inspection, Meade?"

"Sorry," he said, "but beauty was made to be admired."

This pleased her, and her full lips pulled into another smile. "Am I beautiful, Meade? You never said so before."

"I think I'm being chivvied into an admission of something," he murmured and lit a cigar.

"All right," she said. "You can get off the hook. When are you going to get married, Meade?"

At one time this frankness would have bothered him, but he knew her well now and she had no way except complete honesty.

"I'm not thinking about it," Meade said. "Got other things on my mind."

She laughed, a small sound that reminded Meade of things he had supposed long forgotten. There was the remembrance of church bells pealing in the summer-evening quiet in the Ohio town where he had been raised. He recalled the deliciousness of cool water after a run with his dog. He pondered this, wondering why she should remind him of his home and childhood.

Reaching out, Amy touched his hand, her palm warm against his. "Meade, every man thinks of a woman and in a different way. But you're the kind that would think of marriage. She won't wait forever, Meade. Have you asked her?"

"You're too serious for being twenty," Bigelow said, but couldn't evade her. "No, I've not asked her, but we have an understanding."

She laughed. "An understanding is fine for some men, but not for you, Meade. Your woman would have to keep the bed warm." She turned away from him and went into the kitchen. "For being late you get the leftovers. I'm closing in an hour. Business is poor."

She set his meal before him and waited until

he had cut the edge from his appetite. When he reached for his coffee, she asked, "Are you staying in town tonight?"

"Yes."

"Waiting for Murray Sinclair?" She studied him gravely. "Is that part of the job, too, Meade?"

"Hardesty won't do anything. He as much as told me so tonight."

"Are you sure about Murray, Meade?"

"To be positive I would have had to see him fire the shot. One of the teamsters says that he recognized Murray. I'm going on that." He finished his meal and laid fifty cents on the counter. "I hear that in Alder Gulch this would have cost me five dollars."

"I've never been there," Amy Falcon said. "Big business gets all the profits here, and to hear them tell it, the money is in circulation, but I know that they eat their meals at home."

He slid off the stool and picked up his hat. "There's a dance tomorrow night," he said. "If everything turns out well, can I count on a couple?"

"I'll be looking forward to it," she said and watched him leave.

Chapter Two

In the middle of the block, Gruen's Hotel was the largest building, a wide two-story structure with a wide upper gallery. Pausing at the desk in the lobby, Meade palmed a small handbell and Allene Gruen came out, a statuesque woman of thirty. Her hair was copper-colored, accenting decidedly green eyes. She wore flowing dresses that accented her figure, for she had arrived at that stage where, having lost one man, she seriously contemplated capturing another.

Meade registered and laid his dollar on the blotter. Allene said, "I haven't seen you for a week or so, Meade. You've been busy?"

"That's an easy way to be," he murmured, and she took a key from a drawer. He dropped the key into his coat pocket and began to turn away, when her voice halted him.

"You ought to have a home, Meade. Hotels cost you a lot of money." She put just the right amount of lure into her voice to make it interesting.

Meade turned back and put his hands on the edge of the desk. "I make a lot of money," he said.

Her full lips turned down in a slight pout. "I only see a dollar or two of it at a time." Her expression changed. "Come up for some coffee?" She didn't wait for his answer, just turned her head and called to a man in the back room. "Amos, take care of things."

Lifting her skirts slightly, she came around the desk and ascended the stairs; Meade followed her to the upper hall, then walked beside her until they came to the unnumbered door that led to her apartment.

Two small lamps on end tables were turned down low, and she motioned for him to sit down. He chose a single chair and crossed his legs. "Sherry?" she asked. "I'm out of coffee."

"That's fine," he said and laid his hat on the floor. He watched her while she poured, and when she faced him, there was a boldness in her eyes that encouraged this inspection.

He covered his thoughts by lifting his glass.

She sat down across from him, pulling her feet beneath her, and studied him. "You like your job, don't you?"

Bigelow's shoulders rose and fell. "It's a living," he admitted.

"You make five thousand dollars a year, don't you?" She smiled. "That's a lot of money."

"You seem to know a lot about me," Meade said and leaned forward. "How much money do I save?"

"Not enough," Allene said. "You need a woman, Meade."

"I have one," he murmured, but she shrugged it aside.

"She will spend the money." Allene got up and refilled her wine glass. "Another?" He shook his head. "Are you going to marry her, Meade?"

"That's twice tonight somebody asked me that," he said. "Is there any hurry?"

"Some women are more impatient than others," Allene said. "I don't think I'd like to wait, if you were mine." She turned her head quickly as a soft knock rattled the door. Crossing over, she said, "Who is it?"

"Amos, ma'am. Mr. Barnum and the others are asking for Mr. Bigelow."

"Tell them in a little while," Allene said and came back. In her eyes there was a marked resentment against this intrusion, but she covered it quickly. "Always something," she said and frowned when Meade rose. "You don't have to go. Not right now."

"Business," Meade said. "Thanks for the wine, Allene."

"Stop in when you're finished," she said.

"If it's not too late," he told her and walked to the door.

"I never look at the clock," she said, and he smiled before going out. At the foot of the stairs, Meade turned right and went down another hall, pausing at the end room to rap on the door. A man's grumbled voice beckoned him, and Meade stepped into a room full of cigar smoke.

He shook hands all around, then went to a

side window and opened it. Lige Barnum sat at the head of a long table, a square man with the definite stamp of cattleman on him. In his youth he had been a powerful man, but time had shrunk him, leaving him wrinkled and well used by life.

Fred Allendale, sitting at Barnum's right, nodded briefly to Meade as the big man pulled up a chair across from him. Next to Allendale, Calvin Olds fingered his mutton-chop whiskers and seemed out of joint in this gathering.

The fourth man, Jules Buckley, was no older than Meade. He leaned on his forearms and chewed on his cigar. On his face was written the bluntness that characterized the man's every move.

Meade said, "Where is Cartwright and Conover?"

"Cartwright can't make it," Allendale said. "I saw him this evening after supper, and he said that he would abide by any suggestion that was agreed upon."

"All right," Meade said, turning his head as the door opened and Dan Conover came in. He hung up his coat and hat and came directly to the table, the lamplight flashing from his diamond stick-pin.

"Let's get this over with," Conover said and sat down at the head of the table.

Meade raised his head and glanced from one to the other. In this group of men sitting around the table was gathered a power that literally encompassed life and death through a quarter of the Territory. Every time he came here, he was struck by this thought and held by it for a moment.

Conover said, "Meade, what are you going to do about Murray Sinclair and his brothers?"

"I haven't decided fully yet," Meade said. "I want to talk to the man."

"No one can talk to that hardhead," Olds said flatly.

"Have you ever tried?" Meade asked and watched the storekeeper flush. Olds opened his mouth to speak, then thought better of it and studied his folded hands.

"Gentlemen," Conover said softly, "the time has come when we must either force the Sinclairs into a cartel agreement or close them down so that they can no longer operate."

"Is that necessary?" Barnum asked.

"For a closed corporation it is," Conover said. He spread his hands. "I am not a mine owner, a cattle raiser, a lumber man. Neither do I own a store or a bank, but I am the representative of the Silver City Land and Trust Company, and as their agent, I must uphold my stockholders' investments." He cleared his throat and went on. "At the very beginning, mining here was a failure, and it failed because one form of business enterprise tried to outdo the other. Barnum, you are the head of the Colorado-Wyoming Cattle Company, but five years ago the cattle raisers were fighting each other over water. Now, with organization, you market all your beef, assured of steady market values, and there is no more trouble. It is true that no one can raise or sell a head of beef in this part of the Territory without belonging to the organization, but I ask you—who is hurt by this cartel?

"Buckley, you were ready to go under from competition when you made cartel agreements with Cartwright and the Silver City Bank. Now you are alone, working at a steady wage, with a sound timbering schedule."

Conover looked around the room. "All of you have grown fat from the profit of this organization. No one can undercut the other because each is a link in a chain. Now I ask you again—can we tolerate the Sinclairs who insist on bucking us?"

Allendale had remained quietly thoughtful. Now he said, "I think the other side is worth airing, gentlemen. Five years ago I overextended myself. I made loans to a lot of people, who in the end couldn't pay them back. They were the small people, the ones who were the competition. At one point, I was on the verge of having a run made on my bank, but through the help of the Silver City Land and Trust Company, a major portion of my bank was taken over.

"That put a lot of small people out of business, when the notes were called in. It meant the end of the boom years and the beginning of the twenty-five-cent haircut. Maybe that was good for a few, but I think it was bad for a lot of others. A man can't open a store in Silver City without going into the Silver City Consolidated Merchants. There's a price attached to that, though—fifty-one per cent of the business, the controlling interest.

"Gentlemen, all of us have mortgaged ourselves to a machine that has grown so big that no one owns it. It is like a headless monster, still thrashing and breaking things, with no way to stop it.

"Personally, I believe Murray Sinclair is fighting for something, an ideal, perhaps. I believe that we are on the edge of a delicate thing and that it should be handled with caution."

"I disagree," Conover said flatly and swung his eyes around the table, spearing each man in turn. "We have gone too far to permit squabbling. The problem, as I see it, is Meade's. I give him free rein to handle it to his own satisfaction."

He stood up then and placed his chair carefully by the table. "I don't believe there is anything more to say, gentlemen." He waited while a soft murmur ran around the table, then clapped his bowler on his head, and the men stood up, gathering their coats and hats.

Conover waited for Meade Bigelow, touching

him lightly on the arm while the others said good night and filed out. "Come over to the house, Meade. We don't see enough of you anymore."

Bigelow took out his watch and opened it, then put it back after a quick glance. "It's late. Perhaps tomorrow."

Conover removed his cigar and laughed. "Business first, eh, Meade? The Great Northern has a champion in you, son." He used the word slyly, accompanied by a quick squeeze on the arm. "Be careful now. Those Sinclairs are a shiftless, tricky lot. If they've killed once they won't hesitate to kill again."

He gave Meade another slap on the shoulder and hurried out. After the door closed, silence was thick in the room, and Meade walked over and closed the window. The door opened, and Amos thrust his head past the edge.

"Excuse me, Mr. Bigelow. I thought they had all gone, and I was just about to put out the lamps."

"I'll do it before I leave," Bigelow murmured.

"Mr. Buckley and Miss Hart are still in the lobby, sir. They're waiting for you."

"Send them in," Bigelow said and snipped the end from his cigar. A moment later, Jules Buckley re-entered the room with Marilee Hart. She was a small girl with dark eyes, and Bigelow smiled when she offered her hand. "Have a chair," Meade said softly. "The gods have departed."

Bigelow, turning away in search of an ashtray, missed the quick exchange of glances between Buckley and the young woman. Settling himself, Meade said, "Something's eating on you, Jules."

"I guess it is," he said and looked at Marilee Hart. "We want out, Meade, but we don't know how to do it."

"I see," Meade murmured. "Can't you buy out?"

"That's no good," Marilee said. "I don't suppose I'm the businessman my father was, Meade, but I can see the handwriting on the wall. I can't pay out good money for something I was swindled out of in the first place."

Meade's head came up, and he stared at her. "Swindled?"

"Take it easy, honey," Buckley murmured. "That's Meade Bigelow—Mr. Big himself."

"Then it's time to tell Mr. Big something," she said. "In the beginning there were five lumbering outfits and ours was the biggest. Somehow the Silver City Consolidated Merchants got control of Cartwright's freight outfit and put the pinch on all of us. Meade, we couldn't hire a wagon or a teamster! When we tried to run our own rigs, there were accidents. The other lumber mills came in, formed a cartel with Cartwright, but we hung on. Finally we were going broke, so we came in—and fifty-one per cent of our assets were taken over."

"Now you're making money," Meade said softly. "What's the matter with that, Marilee?"

"We're not making money," Buckley said. "That part of it goes to someone else. The Rocky Mountain Lumber Company is on paper, Meade. A figurehead for someone else."

"Cartwright?"

"I thought so for a long time," Buckley said. "His closed concern blocked us out and forced us into this cartel in the first place, but when I talked to him, I didn't get anywhere. He can't do anything, because he don't own his own freight line."

Meade straightened in his chair and gnawed on his cigar. "Who does own it?"

Marilee's slim shoulders rose and fell. "I don't know, Meade. He's in the same canoe we're in. Business is good, but he doesn't see much of the profits. They go somewhere else."

"I see," Meade said and snuffed out his smoke. "This still doesn't tell me why you want out, Marilee. What could you do? Your market for mining stumping and lumber would vanish like a puff of smoke. You'd be right back where you were before—no wagons, no teamsters, no nothing."

"I don't care," Marilee said flatly, and her dark eyes were intense. "I want to fight this thing, Meade. I want to see the day when a man can try his luck and make it or break it on his own efforts. If he makes a million, then the prize is his, not sucked down some long tunnel to the pocketbook of a man we don't even know."

"Now you're talking like Murray Sinclair," Meade murmured.

"Maybe I am," Marilee said. "Sometimes he makes more sense than all the rest of you put together."

"Murray's talk might get him in trouble," Meade said softly.

The young woman shook her head. "I heard about the killing, and Murray didn't do it."

"I have a man that says he saw Murray," Meade said.

"Your man is lying, Meade."

Buckley tugged at her arm. "Let's go, Marilee. Mr. Big won't listen."

She stood up. "Sometime he will want to listen and no one will speak to him." She took Buckley's arm, and they went out. Meade sat at the table for a few minutes, then rose and snuffed out the lamps before leaving.

When Meade stepped to the boardwalk, the traffic had thickened considerably. Miners and lumber men cruised along the walks and filled Karen's Saloon with their wild calling and laughter.

Two blocks over, on an unlighted back street, men moved back and forth in a continuous line, for along this street sat the anonymous houses

31

with drawn shades and no light showing, save a small lamp by the door.

Walking down Lode, Meade turned off to the side street and Dan Conover's house. The colored maid let him in and took his hat, ushering him immediately into the parlor.

June Conover rose from the settee, putting aside her magazine. She gave him a brief kiss and took his arm. "We'll have to be quiet. Mother has had another of her spells, and noise disturbs her."

"Of course," Meade said and sat beside her.

Upstairs, bedsprings protested sharply and a woman's piping voice said, "Clara, who was that?" The colored woman's voice was a soft run of words, and the bedsprings squeaked again, then grew quiet.

June had been listening. She murmured, "Mother worries when Father is out. Her being an invalid is not easy on either of them, especially since it has lasted eighteen years." She gave him a glance and sensed his uneasiness at this confidence. "Meade, you're one of the family now. I want you to know."

"Was it an accident?" he asked.

"Yes," she said. "I was a little girl. There was an argument—they've never seemed too happy together—then Mother tried to run away. We were back East then; Father was with a New York bank. Anyway, the buggy upset and she injured her back."

"I'm sorry," he said.

"Thank you, Meade," June said and squeezed his arm. "She *has* been a trial, but what can one do?" She uncrossed her legs and stood up. "Can I fix you a drink?"

"I'll have to go along," he said. "I wanted to have a talk with your father. Business."

"Always business," she said and came against him, her arms around him. "One of these times I'm going to send Clara on a long errand and see if I can make you forget about business."

"That's too tempting," Meade said and moved away from her.

He retrieved his hat from the hall tree, kissed her again, and went down the darkened path. At the corner he paused, wondering whether he should look for Dan Conover or let it go until tomorrow. Arcing a match, he glanced at his watch, and noting the late hour, decided to sleep on it.

He walked rapidly toward the hotel and entered. The clerk was in the kitchen, and Meade went up the stairs, inserted his key in the lock, and stepped inside. Before he closed the door he glanced out and saw the marshal enter the lobby, take a quick look around, then ascend the stairs without noise. At the unnumbered door of Allene Gruen's room, the marshal rapped lightly twice, then stood there, glancing both ways until the door opened and he stepped inside.

Meade closed his door carefully and lighted the lamp on the small bedside table. His long lips were thoughtful as he removed his clothes and settled for the night.

Heavy Pearl was not heavy; the name was a throwback to a time in Kansas before the war when she threw a drunk down a flight of hotel stairs.

She was in a business that became everyone's sooner or later, but she was a closed-mouthed woman; she knew a great deal and said nothing. In her house, there were two doors, but the back one was reserved for only a select few.

The bottom floor, rear, was her apartment, and here she entertained. On the stairs leading to the top floor of the house, boots made a steady thump, but in the rear, the sound was muted and far away.

After ten, a special key was inserted into the lock, and the back door opened, then closed immediately. She got up and walked into the back hall, where one lamp bathed the doorway feebly. At forty, Heavy Pearl was a handsome woman, a little plump, but still possessing a fine figure. Her hair had been alternately blond, dark, and red. Now it was natural, a rich auburn with a pale streak of gray running through it.

She smiled and touched Dan Conover on the arm and said, "I was wondering if you would come."

"I always do," he said, and they linked arms, walking into Pearl's parlor. She poured him a drink while he removed his coat and ascot tie. When he had settled himself comfortably, she handed him the drink and perched on the arm of his chair.

"Someday you're going to make a mistake, Dan."

He sipped his drink, a thin smile on his lips. "I've made a lot of them," he said, "but the idea is always to have another man handy to take the blame."

She studied him carefully. He was not a handsome man. His face was slightly waspish, his eyes close-set, with the eternal moneyshine in their depths.

"I heard about Murray Sinclair," Pearl said. "This could back up on you and catch your toes in the crack."

He laughed and set his drink aside. Pulling her across his lap, he held her away from him and said, "Pearl, you're always wanting something you can't have. That's bad for you."

"That's right," she admitted. "Why do I put up with you, Dan?"

"Money?" he suggested.

This angered her, and she shoved herself away from him. "I don't like that kind of talk," she snapped. "Once I believed that money could buy what I wanted, but my wants have changed. Now

I want to walk down the street in the daylight and not have other women turn their heads. That's a small thing, Dan, but I want it bad."

"You can't have that," Conover said. "We're both a substitute, Pearl. I'm the man you need and can never have in marriage. You're the woman I want, alive, warm, and not a cripple, but I can't really have you either." He paused to refill his glass. "The talk's too serious. You know I come here to live."

"Yes," Pearl said and listened to the muted thump of boots on the front stairs. "They all do."

Chapter Three

The first bar of morning sunlight cast through the window woke Meade Bigelow, and he dressed carefully before going downstairs to the street.

Bloom was opening his shop, and Meade settled into the chair for his shave. The town was quiet at this early hour, and the only movement along the street was a swamper sweeping the saloon porch, pushing the residue of a fast night into the gutter in rank clouds.

After his shave, Meade walked down the street and crossed over, for he had observed smoke spiraling from the chimney in Amy Falcon's Restaurant. He entered and found that he was the only customer.

The wall clock showed the time to be six-thirty.

Amy peered around the partition and said, "Did you stay up all night, or are you an early riser?" She came to the counter, spreading silverware. When she sniffed the Bay Rum she smiled. "I think it's symbolic, Meade—you don't stay still long enough to own a razor."

"Wheatcakes, steak, and eggs," he said. "Put some potatoes on the plate, too."

"I hope your woman can cook," Amy murmured and went into the kitchen. He listened to pans bang on the stove, then she came back. "Come on back so I won't have to shout."

He smiled and skirted the end of the counter. She slid a chair up to a table, and he sat down. She laid out more silverware, then turned her attention to the stove and his meal. After she placed the platter on the table, she sat down across from him and watched him eat.

After his second cup of coffee, she said, "Marilee and Buckley came over to my cabin last night." She waited until he raised his eyes to hers, then added, "Meade, can't you help them?"

"Help them what?" he asked. "Amy, I don't own Rocky Mountain Lumber, nor do I dictate policy to Great Northern." He crossed to the stove for a refill on the coffee. When he sat down, he took a sip then pushed the cup aside. "Seven years ago, the mines were here—everything was here, but all chopped up. Everybody owned something and was trying to hook the other fellow. Fred Allendale thought there was going to be a big boom and made a lot of loans. Almost everyone was indebted to his bank.

"Then Dan Conover came along, a sharp operator from the East, and he tried to awake Allendale to the shaky financial position he had gotten himself into, but it was too late. Because he had faith in the country and its development, he lent Fred Allendale, who owned the bank, twenty thousand dollars, but somehow word got out that Allendale was in trouble and people, the depositors, began a run. Conover held off as long as he could, then told Allendale that he would have to withdraw the loan. Of course, that would break Fred, so Conover, through his connections back East, formed the Silver City Land and Trust Company. The financial backing was from the East, but Dan was in charge. Through this company, he bought Allendale out of the red, and in turn, took a two-thirds partnership in the bank.

"Of course, he had to call in all the outstanding paper that Allendale had out, and in consequence, most of the small outfits went under. The first to go were the merchants, but through the Trust Company, Conover organized them under the Silver City Consolidated Merchants."

"For fifty-one per cent of their business," Amy said.

"He is a businessman who answers to the stock-holders," Meade said patiently. "Amy, a cartel was the only thing because of his investment. He had to protect it, and the only way was through a corporation to keep out competition."

"What about Cartwright Freighting Company?" Amy asked. "Did he owe money also?"

"They all did," Meade said, "but the freighters—and I think there were five or six different outfits—decided to up their prices and bought heavily. When they came here to sell, the merchants refused to buy. For a few weeks there was some bad feeling, then Conover met with them and offered to pull them out by a cartel with the Merchants. The wagons and property were pooled, and Cartwright headed the company."

"Now tell me about Marilee Hart's lumber company."

"Don't get in a hurry," Meade told her. "So far, these cartels were controlled through Allendale's bank, now called the Silver City Bank. But that is owned by Silver City Land and Trust. Conover, acting in the interest of his stockholders, had to force the others into cartel agreement to survive. By closing off store credit and stopping the freight wagons, he forced the lumber men to combine, and Marilee Hart was to head the Rocky Mountain Lumber Company after her father was killed."

"And all this was done without firing a shot." Amy Falcon shook her head sadly. "Meade, it's not right. Conover has the complete say-so over everything."

"Not exactly," Meade said. "He represents a board back East which makes the decisions. Be grateful to him, Amy, because he's a smart man and this country would be a mess now if it wasn't for his financial genius."

"Did the cattlemen come into this—whatever you called it—cartel, or were they pushed into it like the others were?"

"That's using the wrong word," Meade said,

"or the wrong meaning. They were forced to do something that was good for them and made them all much better off financially. Through the Silver City cartels, Conover was able to close both the buying and selling market. They had to go in or go under. He held paper on their land and herds, and it was sell and pay the money back or refuse to form a cartel and lose the land anyway. The end was the contract forming the Colorado-Wyoming Cattle Company.

"By use of the same tactics, the small mine owners were forced to capitulate and the Great Northern was formed." He smiled. "That's when I came into the picture. The rest of this I've pieced together bit by bit."

"Not a pretty picture, is it?" She studied his blunt face.

"Amy, I don't fully understand what you have against Great Northern. The whole country depends on its output and the cartelled industries controlled by Great Northern interests. How can that be bad?"

"You just said it—the whole country depends on Great Northern for the breath of life. That's a bad thing, Meade. When everyone owns a little piece, a man can fail and not hurt anyone. What would happen if Murray Sinclair broke this monopoly, Meade?"

He sat up straight in his chair, and for a moment there was silence between them. "So that's what

Murray is trying to do?" He slapped the table. "Amy, I love you."

She had grown pale, and her knuckles were white as they gripped the edge of the table. "Damn," she said softly, then added, "Meade, I don't think I like you."

He dipped a hand into his pocket and laid fifty cents on the table, but she brushed it onto the floor where it rolled under the stove. "The meal was on me, Meade. I like Great Northern money less every day."

"Amy," he said softly, "what are you afraid of?"

She stood up quickly and placed a hand under his left armpit, feeling the hard outlines of his .44 Colt. "That's what I'm afraid of, that you'll kill Murray, who is our only chance for a different way, other than what Great Northern tells us."

His temper slipped, and a hard edge of anger appeared. "Dammit, I'm just the general super. I didn't buy up the controlling stock from the Land and Trust Company. That was a deal between Conover and a private financier."

"I'm not blaming you, Meade, only I just don't see how a thing like that could happen. No one understands."

He took a cigar from his pocket and fired it. "Suppose that Great Northern owed the Trust Company a million dollars and the Trust Company owned the voting share of Great Northern. After a few years of mining and paying

42

interest on the loan, Great Northern, which is really the Trust Company, has amassed enough assets to pay off the loan of a million dollars.

"Actually, the money is owed to oneself, the Trust Company, so on paper, there is a transfer of ownership, the assets transferred, and the debt canceled. Great Northern Mining and Smelting is the big boss then."

"And you're the one who drives this great big machine around, aren't you?"

"I only execute company policy," Meade said flatly.

"And now you're going to execute Murray Sinclair with a gun." She turned away from him. "There's always the gun when paper fails, isn't there?"

"I don't know what you're getting so damned mad about," Meade said. "Big business is a ruthless game, and the stakes get pretty high. A man was murdered, Amy. I didn't want that, but since it's happened, I'll make sure it doesn't happen again." He picked up his hat and moved to the archway. "We're heading for a big fight, Amy, and I don't want that."

"Neither do I," Amy Falcon said. "You'd better go, Meade. I have work to do."

"Sure," he murmured and went outside.

Across the street, Meade took a chair on the hotel gallery and hoisted his feet to the rail. From the end of the street, two riders nodded and came

43

on. They dismounted one building up. Clymer and Garroway walked toward Meade; Clymer had a .44 Evans repeating rifle tucked in the crook of his arm.

Pausing by the porch step, Clymer said, "We'll be around, Mr. Bigelow."

"I'll let you know if I need you," Bigelow said and watched them cross to the saloon. Clymer was the one he focused on, for in the man there was a broad streak of meanness. Bigelow had seen it come out at odd times—against an unruly horse, a stubborn man. Garroway stayed in the shadows, never speaking, but he wore a gun in a cross-draw holster and Meade suspected the man was fast.

At eight o'clock, Meade checked his watch against the sun and pulled the hat lower over his eyes. Jim Hardesty, the marshal, came from the jail and walked toward the hotel. He saw Meade on the porch and mounted the steps to take the chair beside the heavy man.

"Good day for trouble," Hardesty said.

"Is it?"

"Let's not play around with each other, Meade," Hardesty said. "I want this to be fair if it comes to trouble."

"It'll be fair," Meade assured him, "if there is trouble. I just want to talk to Murray." He shot Hardesty a long glance. "I was looking for you last night around eleven."

"Making my rounds," Hardesty said smoothly. "I went to the jail around one and didn't leave. A quiet night." He rolled a smoke with great care. "Anything important, Meade?"

"Nothing important," Meade murmured and swung his head to look up and down the street. Dan Conover came around the far corner, June on his arm, her parasol lifted against the fresh sunlight. Conover nodded in passing, and June flashed Meade a quick smile; then Conover unlocked the small office of the Silver City Land and Trust Company and went inside.

June paused in the doorway, looking back at Meade for an inviting moment. Hardesty stared at her with a frank interest, then said, "How do you do it, Meade?"

When he got no answer, Hardesty rose and shied his cigaret into the street. "Let's make this a peaceful day," he said and walked back toward the jail.

Meade sat there, a big, idle man, and at ten-thirty, his attention sharpened as three horsemen rode the length of Lode Street and dismounted by the hardware store.

They saw Meade and crossed over, then ducked under the hitchrail to stand by the base of the porch. Murray Sinclair was taller than Meade Bigelow, although not as heavy. He had pale hair and dark eyes, a startling combination in a freckled face. Sam and Reilly remained by the edge of the walk, placing a heavy interest on Meade.

Bracing a foot against the bottom step, Murray said, "Meade, friend, I was hoping to catch you."

"Why?" Bigelow asked bluntly. "Is something bothering you?"

"A drink, maybe," said Murray. "I've got a hell of a thirst. Maybe a little talk or a laugh or two."

"Let's skip the drink and get on with the talk," Meade said and watched the dancing mischief in Murray's dark eyes. The man wore a loud green shirt, wash-faded jeans, and a black hat with a foot-high crown. He wore a gun, a .44 Smith & Wesson, in a cutaway holster.

"Heard that you've been away, Murray." Meade's voice was soft and even.

"I move around a lot," Murray said and laughed. He was the kind of man who laughed at anything, for he never took life too seriously.

"One of my men claims that he saw you, Murray." Meade left his chair and moved to the edge of the porch.

Sinclair's shoulders rose and fell. "A lot of men see me, Meade." He tilted his head back and squinted. "I heard about it, Meade. Are you accusing me?"

"Not yet," Meade said flatly. "When I do, you won't have any doubts. You want to tell me where you were, Murray?"

"Great Northern don't have a ring in my nose,"

Sinclair said. "Go to hell, Meade. Make any talk about me and you'll get roughed up."

The fun went out of Sinclair's eyes, leaving sharp splinters of temper in them. He waited a moment longer, then turned on his heel. After motioning for his brothers to follow him, he stomped across the street to the saloon, his hard-driving heels puffing up small bombs of dust.

Lige Barnum came out of the hotel, and Meade turned his head to see who it was. Barnum teetered on the heels of his run-over boots and nibbled on the soggy end of an unlighted cigar. He said, "For a minute I thought you was goin' to be a damn fool and tackle all three of 'em."

"I might have made it," Meade murmured. "Murray doesn't seem worried."

"He's worried," Barnum said. "He's been worried a long time, but he's proud. He won't bend to a man no matter what. Look how long he's held out. He'd cart that ore to Denver on his back before he'd give an inch to Great Northern."

"Whose side are you on?" Meade asked quietly.

Barnum lifted two coins from his pocket. "They're silver. It's as sound a god as I can think of at the moment. Tried this idealist way once, Meade, and damned near went broke. Seems funny to me that Murray ain't gone bust. Must be getting enough out of that mine of his to make ends meet, although there can't be much profit in it by the time he hauls that ore to Denver."

47

"There's twenty thousand dollars profit floating around someplace," Meade said. "Who do you think got it, Lige?"

"I wouldn't even guess," Barnum said. "I like to play the safest games. You can have the touch-and-go ones."

He moved past Bigelow and crossed the street to the saloon. After Barnum disappeared inside the swinging doors, Bigelow turned and went back to his chair. His feet elevated to the railing, he passed the time until noon by watching the people move up and down the street.

When the hands of his watch were vertical, he left the porch and entered Amy Falcon's Restaurant. The counter was full, and she motioned for him to go into the back room. A young boy helped her with the trade, splitting his time between counter and kitchen, and when all the orders were filled, she left him and came into the back room.

Meade had helped himself and was half finished with his meal. Amy frowned and said, "Why eat stew? I would have fixed you a steak." She smiled and sat down, stretching her long legs. "I was watching through the front window while you teased the hornet's nest. Murray looked mad when he crossed the street."

"A little put out," Meade admitted.

She leaned forward and said, "June Conover might not like what you're doing, Meade?"

He lifted his eyes and looked at her. "What am I doing, Amy?"

For a moment, Amy Falcon knew the confusion people feel when they misjudge the privileges of friendship and say too much, and at the same time, say too little.

"It's really none of my business, Meade."

"Make it your business," he invited.

Biting her lower lip, Amy turned the words over in her mind. "I don't think she would like to see you roll in the dirt, Meade. A fight is for a common man, and she wants something more than common. She wants security, and there's nothing secure about you. You're as proud as Murray and just as stubborn. You like to be right, Meade, which is fine, but she likes to be right, too. I don't think it's going to work."

"That's being honest anyway, isn't it?"

"My mouth is too big," Amy said and began to stand, but he put his hand out and halted her movement. "I really should help Ralphie, Meade."

"Sit down," he told her gently. "There's no one like you, Amy. You're blunt and honest, and I can always count on it. Do me a favor and tell me when I get off the track. Sometimes a man can't see it until it's too late."

"All right," she said, "but remember that you asked me."

She turned her head as a man's voice rose in

49

the dining room; then Ralphie came in, his eyes round and worried. "Mr. Bigelow, I think Mr. Sinclair wants to talk to you."

"I'll go out," Meade said and started to rise, but Amy's hand came out and took his sleeve.

"Wait! Ralphie, ask Murray to come on back." When the boy went out, she added, "No use arguing in front of a crowd."

Murray stepped through the arch, and on his face there was no ready smile. His one glance at Amy Falcon showed his annoyance at her presence, but he offered no suggestion that she leave.

Murray asked, "Are you looking for a fight, Meade?"

"Did I say that?"

Murray made a cutting motion with his hand. "Don't start fancy talkin' me, Meade. I don't want to listen to it. You'd like to blame me for killing Goofy Harris, wouldn't you?"

"Only if you're guilty," Meade said calmly. "Then, if Jim Hardesty didn't arrest you, I'd shoot you myself."

"My business is my own," Murray said flatly. "I don't have to account to Great Northern for anything I do or where I've been."

"This time you do," Meade said. "Don't make me get tough, Murray, and I will if I have to."

"Don't rub my face in anything! I don't have to take any crap off of you or the bunch you work for!"

"Now you just do what's convenient for you," Meade said. "But one way or another, Murray, I'm going to get this settled. You'll save some trouble if you come off that damned high horse of independence and tell me where you were."

"Keep your damned mouth shut about me," Sinclair warned. "I'll blow a hole through you before I'll knuckle down to Great Northern law." He whirled on his heel and stalked out.

"There goes trouble," Amy said softly.

"All he has to do is to tell me where he was," Meade said patiently. "Am I being unreasonable, Amy?"

"No," she said. "Meade, can't you see his point?"

"All I can see is twenty thousand in company silver missing," Meade said and put on his hat. He glanced at her, and her smooth face was grave. He reached out and brushed a strand of golden hair from her forehead, and it was as soft as unpicked cotton.

He turned away from her and left the restaurant, crossing the street to the Silver City Land and Trust Company.

Chapter Four

When Meade entered the Trust Company office, he found the outer room vacant and pushed the swinging gate that separated this small space. Dan Conover's private office was in the rear, a paneled room with a carved mahogany desk and plush chairs.

June was seated at a small table flanked by huge filing cabinets and a safe; she turned her head as he entered. "Meade! I didn't hear you come in."

He put his arms around her when she stood up and kissed her soundly. "How's the chief book-keeper?"

She wrinkled her nose at him. "I'd rather be settled in my own kitchen, baking cherry pie for you."

"Cherries are out of season," Meade smiled. "Anyway, I think you'd like a hired woman to do the cooking."

Cocking her head to one side, June murmured, "Darling, I don't know whether you're paying me a compliment or teasing me."

"I meant it kindly," he said and wondered how he got so quickly onto the thinner ice.

Her smile reassured him that he was safe. "I don't like unkind things," June said and took his arm, leading him to a soft chair. He sat down, and she perched on the arm, leaning against him.

Meade said, "Someone might come in."

She laughed about it and touched his lips with her fingertips. "Impropriety is inexcusable only if you get caught. I think people are crude when they let themselves get caught." She glanced at the large wall clock and got off the chair arm. "Father is a punctual man, and he'll be coming back in a minute. Meade, you have some powder on your cheek."

"Oh," Meade said and wiped it off. This caused him to smile slightly, and he added, "Isn't a trace of powder permissible when we're engaged?"

"Father is a moralist," June murmured and shot him a mischievous glance. "But even his strict code of ethics can be surmounted." She stopped talking and went back to her desk quickly.

Dan Conover came into the room a scant moment after she had reseated herself. He seemed pleasantly surprised to see Meade and offered his hand before hanging up his hat.

"I've been observing with interest," he said, "the way you handled that troublemaker Sinclair. Very nicely done, my boy. He's worried now, and I think he'll break himself if you give him the rope."

Conover settled himself behind his desk, for he was a man who always talked better with imposing furniture around him. "Meade, I don't presume to advise you, but I've asked Fred Allendale and Lige Barnum to act as go-betweens in this matter."

"I can handle it," Meade said, offended somehow and not quite able to pin it down.

"Of course you can," Conover said and waved his hand. "But Murray is a hothead who plots the downfall of Great Northern to gain his own ends. We can't have that, can we? I think more will be accomplished if we use disinterested go-betweens here, rather than have you two meet head-on over this issue. There are times when careful negotiations will produce quicker results than open battle."

"Are you advising me as Chairman of the Board of Great Northern?" Meade asked.

Conover smiled. "I am a prospective father-in-law advising a very good friend. I have your welfare at heart, Meade, believe me. I don't think a man of your position should stoop to open brawling before the public, and Murray is drinking heavily now, trying to work himself up to a fight." He glanced at his daughter. "My dear, would you step out and ask Mr. Allendale and Mr. Barnum to come in?"

After she went out, Meade said, "You seemed sure that I would listen, didn't you?"

"Of course," Conover said softly. "You're intelligent, Meade, and intelligent men respond to reason." He stood up as Allendale and Barnum entered, and shook hands with each man in turn. "Glad you could spare the time, gentlemen."

Allendale seemed in a quiet mood, but Barnum spoke with his habitual bluntness. "Dan has been talking to us, Meade, and we don't want trouble in Silver City. Murray's takin' on the booze and gettin' ready to call you."

"Fight or no fight," Meade said, "I want to know where Murray was when Goofy was killed. You tell him I said so."

"We'll do our best, Meade, if you'll stay away from him."

"You may be sticking your nose in where it'll get burned," Meade said.

"That's our decision and our lookout," Allendale said. "Go to the hotel and wait, Meade. We'll talk to Murray for you." He waited until Meade nodded, then turned and went out, Barnum following him. Meade waited a moment, glanced at Conover and June, then put on his hat and left the building.

He took his seat on the hotel porch and waited. For the better part of an hour he sat in thoughtful silence, pestered by this wasteful idleness.

When a woman's heels tapped the floor, Meade turned his head slightly, and Allene Gruen sat down beside him. She had on a pale-blue dress that fit her tightly around the waist and breasts. Her arms were bare, and she offered him a ready smile.

"You didn't come back," she murmured. "I think you like to make people wait, Meade."

"Business before pleasure," he said and watched her eyes grow round with interest.

"I said nothing about pleasure," Allene murmured, smiling slightly.

"A beautiful woman is always a pleasure," Meade said, and her smile deepened. He extracted a cigar from his shirt pocket and scissored the end with his teeth. When he got it going, he settled back in the chair, ribbons of gray smoke rising past his face.

Across the street, Clymer and Garroway came out of the mercantile and stood against the wall, their hats pulled low on their foreheads. Clymer still cradled his .44 Evans repeating rifle and lifted a finger toward Meade, pulling his attention away after this brief signal.

"There's a bad one," Allene said softly. "You have strange friends, Meade."

"No friend," Meade said. "He works for Great Northern, the same as I do." He glanced across the street, for Fred Allendale and Lige Barnum came from the saloon, blinking their eyes against the strong sunlight. For a moment they chatted, shooting glances toward the hotel porch.

Meade said, "They're waiting for you to leave."

"You're very blunt," Allene murmured and stood up, her dress rustling softly.

"Only in business," Meade told her and

watched a smile start at the ends of her full lips.

"Ah," she said and went inside. Allendale and Barnum immediately crossed the street.

Allendale did the talking. "He's willing to let the whole thing slide, Meade, but he wants to know what you meant by your remarks. Were you accusing him of shooting Goofy and holding up the wagon?"

"I meant exactly what I said," Meade told him. "Tell him to take it any way it suits his fancy."

"Oh, come on now, Meade," Allendale urged. "That's no good and you know it. Murray's had a few drinks, and he's getting surly. Sam and Reilly have agreed to stay out of it, and I think we can smooth this over if you'll explain exactly what you meant."

"The point in Murray's mind is whether you accused him of the killing." Barnum glanced at Allendale after this speech.

"Did it sound as though I was?"

"We're not the ones to judge," Allendale said, trying to remain neutral in this matter. "Meade, if you're so sure, you should have accused him outright and had done with it."

"If I was sure," Meade said, "I wouldn't be sitting here. I'd be after Murray." He glanced at Barnum. "What does Murray think?"

"He's put out as hell," Barnum said. "He claims that you accused him in a roundabout way and wants satisfaction for it."

"What does he call satisfaction?"

"An apology or a fight," said Allendale. "He wants out from under the charge or to be tried for it." Allendale gnawed on a cold cigar. "Meade, what are you trying to do?"

"Find out where Murray was," Meade said. "The man's so damn proud he won't give an inch for the devil himself. He came to the restaurant while I was eating, shooting his mouth off. He's got it in for Great Northern, and he's getting stubborn about it. I can be just as stubborn."

The two men looked at each other, shrugged their shoulders, and walked back to the saloon.

Settling back in his rocker, Meade thought about it. He understood Murray well and knew the man would pick his words apart because Meade represented Great Northern, the man's all-consuming hate.

Even when Garvey swore that he had seen Murray, Bigelow was reluctant to believe it, because Murray was not the kind of man who would kill. The man's patience was short at best and he liked to fight, but a killing was not in Murray's line.

Because of his position with Great Northern, Meade had to protect the company interests, and because of this, he had to be doubly sure that he had the right man.

Glancing across the street, Meade saw Clymer and Garroway against the building. He whistled softly, and their heads came up; when he beckoned, they crossed the street.

"Murray's making big talk at Karen's," Clymer said.

"What're Sam and Reilly doing?" Meade asked.

"Nothing," Clymer murmured. He wore his hat low over his eyes and had the habit of tipping his head back to look at a man. "They'll follow Murray, you can bet on that."

"See that Sam and Reilly mind their own business in case anything breaks," Meade said. He glanced across the street as Allendale and Barnum came out again. "Get lost," he told them, "but not too far lost."

"We'll be around," Clymer said and went back across the dust to take up his place along the mercantile wall.

Allendale still gnawed on the sour end of his dead cigar, while Barnum wore a worried expression. Bigelow shifted his chair away from the railing because the sun was dropping rapidly now and a strong light scalded him. Another two hours and darkness would fall.

Running a finger around his collar, Lige Barnum said, "Murray says he never would have made those remarks if it hadn't been for what you said, Meade. He says that you're accusing him of this because it's Great Northern's way of squeezing him into an agreement. He says that he's willing to let the thing drop and he meant nothing by his remarks in the restaurant if you meant nothing by yours."

"What if I agree to that?" Meade asked.

"Then it's ended," Allendale said with a great deal of hope.

"I don't agree," Meade said flatly and watched the irritation cross Barnum's face.

"He claims that you started it deliberately," Barnum said. "He's convinced it's a Great Northern plot and he's willing to forget it, but he wants your apology first."

"Tell him that Great Northern doesn't accept threats from anyone," Meade said.

"Jesus!" Barnum said heatedly. He calmed himself and added, "Meade, this pussyfooting is only making him sore as a boil. One of you better give in before he comes out and settles it himself."

"That's what I've been waiting for," Bigelow said blandly.

Barnum rolled his eyes toward the heavens as though he expected divine guidance or was expressing the ultimate in disgust. Allendale removed the cigar from his mouth and said, "Meade, can't you understand how Murray feels? One show of weakness and Great Northern will gobble him in one mouthful. Personally, I don't think he shot Goofy or was even near that ore wagon when it was robbed."

"Then let him say where he was and we'll forget it."

"He can't do that," Allendale pointed out. "You know he can't. A long time ago he planted his flag against Great Northern and ever since he's been hauling his ore in spite of every attempt to block him out."

"It seems to me," Meade said, "that Murray is testing his muscles against me to see how far Great Northern will back up. I can tell you now that it's not a goddam inch!"

"I give up," Barnum said and plucked a cigar from his vest pocket, snipping off the end with a sudden vising of his jaws. He snapped a match on his thumbnail, then lit the cigar and puffed so furiously that he began to cough.

"I'll tell him that Great Northern is not accusing him, that you just want to know where he was at the time of the robbery. Is that all right, Meade?" Allendale's voice was filled with hope.

"Tell him what I just said," Meade murmured and pulled his hat low to shield his eyes from the glare of the setting sun.

"Isn't there any give in you at all?" Barnum asked, near the end of his patience.

"Not much," Meade admitted. "That isn't a surprise to you, is it, Lige?"

"I guess not," admitted Barnum. "We'll go and tell him what you said." Turning, he walked back to the saloon, Allendale following with his head down, deep in thought.

Thinking about it, Meade decided that somewhere he had made a mistake and wondered how he could get around it. Although he had guarded against it, Murray had forced him into a position where he had to defend Great Northern.

Murray was obscuring the real issue with the fight between himself and the cartels. In his own mind, Meade could find no blame for what Murray believed, but business did not often take into consideration the small man's dream.

Across the street, Amy Falcon came to the door of her restaurant and stood there. They looked at each other for a long moment, and then she turned and went back inside, but the impression of her remained in Meade's mind. Amy Falcon sometimes troubled him, for she was too much like him for comfort. Often she left him with the impression that she read his thoughts, and at times he caught himself trying to guard them from her.

Meade had often wondered what there was about Amy that interested him, for she was not at all like June Conover. There was animosity between these two, and June resented Amy Falcon with an intensity that Meade did not fully understand.

He had never given June reason for jealousy, but it showed clearly when anger made her mask slip. Trying to rationalize it, Meade came to the conclusion that Amy's beauty overshadowed June's to the degree that June felt inferior. Amy's voluptuousness, coupled with the bold way she had of looking at a man—not suggestive but meeting him on his terms—set other women against her.

Steps rattled the loose boards of the walk, and Meade interrupted his thoughts as June and her father came toward the hotel. They stopped and Conover said, "Nothing yet?"

"No," Meade murmured. "He thinks I'm trying to push him into a deal."

"Keep at it," Conover said. "Come to supper, Meade."

"Not tonight," Meade murmured and saw June's lips pull down in a small pout. He smiled with his eyes and said, "I was thinking about you."

This erased her expression, and she returned his smile. "How nice," she said and took her father's arm, walking on down the street.

Meade settled back in his chair and waited.

Chapter Five

The sun was well down, and long shadows began to stretch into the street, almost reaching the boardwalk on the hotel side. Some of the pedestrian traffic thinned out, and the quit whistle blew at the mine, its echo slamming among the hills until it died out.

Shifting to ease a kink in his back, Meade saw Barnum and Allendale leave the saloon. Allendale paused to light his cigar, and they crossed the street to where Meade waited.

Barnum said, "He's got his ears back, Meade. He thinks that Great Northern is trying to push him around. I suggest that you back off now and let the marshal handle any formal complaint you want to make."

"You won't get anywhere with Murray personally," Allendale added. "He sees you as the big gun up on the hill and will be automatically hostile to anything you say."

"I can't let this go by," Meade said flatly. "Tell him I'll let this go when he tells me what happened to the stolen goods off the ore stages."

"My God!" Allendale said. "What a thing to throw on a fire. Meade, I ask you again to be lenient here. Murray is a hothead, and he's fighting shadows. We know Murray and don't expect too much of him, but we're counting on you to be level-headed about it."

"I'm sorry," Meade said, "but I have a job to do. The silver is gone and a man is dead. Someone has to answer for it."

Allendale frowned. "I don't like to see Great Northern acting as the law in Silver City, Meade."

Bigelow straightened in his chair. "You want me to back up just because Murray doesn't like it?" He shook his head. "I represent Great Northern and if I back up one inch now, do you think I'll ever be able to stop backing? Sorry, gentlemen. Tell Murray what I said about the robbery."

Allendale and Barnum looked at each other. Barnum said, "We're only the go-betweens here, so let's get back." The banker nodded, and they recrossed the street.

In her restaurant, Amy Falcon moved around the walls, lighting lamps with a taper. The sun was completely gone now, and the mountains pulled the remaining light down, shattering its bold colors into blood-red pennants that ran to the ends of the horizons and beyond.

A door down from Amy's restaurant, Clymer and Garroway sagged against the wall. Clymer had his short-barreled Evans repeater nestled in the crook of his arm, and he lifted his hand, waved at Meade, then let it drop, his attention never wavering from the saloon door.

Lonigan went around the saloon, lighting the lamps to push back the night, and Murray Sinclair came out and stood on the boardwalk. He swayed a little, staggered when he walked, but his mind was honed to a singleness of purpose. Behind the swinging doors, Sam and Reilly Sinclair waited, coming out when Murray stepped into the street and crossed over.

Watching him, Meade saw that Murray walked with the studied cautiousness of a man who has had too much to drink and knows it. Halting by the hotel steps, Murray said, "So you finally came out with it. I won't stand for that kind of talk, Meade. Great Northern is pushing me too damned far now."

"I have a man that saw you, Murray," Bigelow said and watched the color drain from Murray's face.

"That's a goddam lie! Let's see you prove it."

"It looks like I'll have to," Meade murmured. "What's the matter with you, Murray? You've fought Great Northern for three years. You know you can't win."

Across the street, Clymer called out in a sharp voice, and when Bigelow looked up, Sam and Reilly were standing flat-footed in the middle of the street, held motionless by the threat of Clymer's rifle.

"It looks like you invited your brothers in on this," Meade said and left the porch. He stopped a few feet from Murray and waited.

Two dozen townsmen appeared as if from nowhere and lined the other side of the street. Bigelow said, "You've traded lead with Great Northern long enough, Murray. We're tired of fighting you just to put you on easy street. So I'll give you a chance. Get on your horse and clear out of the country. Take your brothers with you. Be smart this time, Murray. Sell out, because my generosity is wearing thin as hell."

"Sure," Murray said softly. "Great Northern, the hog, wants it all one way or another." He swayed a little. "I'm drunk, you know that? You know why I get drunk? I'll tell you why. I got a rich mine, but can I get my ore out? No! Great Northern has the ore wagons tied up. Three wagons at a time, that's the way I haul it. Sittin' there with a rifle to keep men like Clymer and Garroway from shootin' me off the seat.

"I can't even buy a sack of beans in Silver City, because I'm not in with Great Northern." Murray made an aimless gesture with his hands. "You're strangling the country, Meade. Milking it dry without putting a nickel back."

"Get out of town, Murray," Meade said. "That's the best I can do for you."

"Sure," Murray said and started to turn away, but never completed his move. Whirling back suddenly, he lashed out, driving Bigelow backward into the porch steps.

Someone shouted, and more men poured from Karen's Saloon, but Meade paid no attention to them. Between being in a hurry and being drunk, Murray missed a kick and fell heavily.

Fred Allendale and Barnum hurried across the street, and Bigelow stepped back, waiting for Murray to regain his feet. Slowly, Murray pushed himself erect, and the crowd waited, the street ominously quiet.

A deep temper filled Murray's eyes, and he faced Meade Bigelow. "The quiet man," he said. "I've always wondered when the day would come when we'd meet."

"The day's arrived," Bigelow told him. "If there's a fight in you, better clear it out of your system now."

"I'm drunk," Murray said. "But I'll be sober pretty soon, Meade. You better get yourself a gun because that's what I'll come after you with."

"That would be a mistake," Meade said, but Murray had already whirled around and was butting his way through the crowd.

Glancing at Bigelow, Allendale said, "We tried, Meade. Have it your own way now." He turned and walked down the street, and the crowd began to thin out rapidly. Meade waited until the street was clear before crossing to Amy Falcon's Restaurant.

It was too early for the miner crowd, and the townsmen ate at home. She nodded toward the back room, and he went around the counter. Amy had set his place, with another across from it. He washed at the sink and sat down.

"Did she invite you for supper?" Amy asked.

"Yes," he murmured.

"For a smart man," she said, "you're not very wise. In an hour this will be all over town—Meade Bigelow turned down supper with the Conovers to eat with the big Swede. Your stock may go down because of it."

He laughed softly, and she set the meal on the table. For a few minutes they ate in silence; then Amy said, "A penny, Meade."

Shrugging his shoulders, he said, "I was thinking just about the ways you've been hurt that I didn't even know about."

"I don't understand," she said. She reached for the lamp and turned it up until the light was strong on their faces.

"What you said a few minutes ago," he murmured.

Amy laughed at his seriousness. "About your stock? I was making a bad joke, Meade."

"I meant your remark about being a big Swede. Careless remarks overheard are sometimes the most painful, because a person knows that wasn't the worst or even all. I think the wondering pains the most."

"Sometimes it does," she said softly and lowered her eyes to her plate. "I find that I don't like the bright light after all," she murmured and turned the lamp down very low. She did not look at him directly, and he understood how much of an effort it could be to smile at times, as she was trying to do now. She was a realist, he decided, a person who always faced the facts, no matter how unpleasant.

"It really doesn't matter about me, Meade." She gave him a quick glance, a test to see if she had her emotions under control. When she found she had, she locked eyes with him and smiled.

"It's always foolish to be stung by something you can't help," she said. "But I'm five-foot-ten and weigh a hundred and forty pounds. There isn't much I can do about that, is there?" She moved her fork in aimless circles through the mashed potatoes. "I suppose I can console myself with the thought that beef is cheap these days and some men believe you can't get too much of a good thing."

"Stop it, Amy!" Meade said. "I've never known you to feel sorry for yourself."

"Well, I am," she admitted. "It's one of the few luxuries left that I can afford under the Great Northern rule." For a moment she fell silent, then added, "Sorry, Meade. Things sort of piled up, that's all."

"It happens to everybody," he said and finished his steak. Studying her, he decided that her beauty was a reflection of some deep, inner warmth. She would brush her blonde hair until it glistened, braid it, wash her face until the sun bounced from it, and be ready to meet anyone. She never pretended to be something that she wasn't.

In contrast, June Conover would keep him waiting while she fussed with her hair or powdered her cheeks. Meade suspected that Amy Falcon would never do that to a man. He considered these two women, trying to decide where the real value lay.

Through girlhood and into her first years of womanhood, the female was schooled in the deception of man, and men liked it. They wanted the mystery during the chase, but after the chase was over—Meade wondered about this.

With a woman too honest to pretend, there was the other extreme. That honesty would intrigue a man, but would it endure through a lifetime together?

Meade did not know, and this bothered him.

Raising her eyes quickly, Amy caught him studying her. She said, "You like to look at me, don't you, Meade?"

The frankness bowled him over for a moment. "Yes, I do. I was thinking how beautiful you are, Amy, without even trying to be." He saw her expression freeze and added quickly, "I didn't say anything wrong, did I?"

"No." Her voice was a small sound. "You never

do, Meade." She added sugar to her coffee and stirred it. "I just don't think June Conover would give you the right to say it, that's all."

"She doesn't own me," said Bigelow.

Amy shook her head. "When a man and woman love each other, that's a form of owning, too." Sipping her coffee, she studied him over the rim of the cup. "If you were mine—" She moved her shoulders. "But you're not." She set the cup down and leaned forward, her voice softly confidential. "I'll let you in on a secret, Meade. I hope to be shot by a jealous wife when I'm eighty."

"You're absolutely shameless," Meade said and laughed.

Finishing his coffee, Meade leaned back in the chair and lit his after-dinner cigar. He listened to the soft sounds coming from the street. The miners came into town at this hour, and the tempo picked up.

The front door of the restaurant opened, and Ralphie came in, his hair glistening and slicked down with water. "Customers will be coming in soon," he said and put on a flour-sack apron.

When the front door opened again, he went out to the dining room to return a moment later with a worried expression in his eyes.

"Mr. Bigelow, Reilly Sinclair is out there. He wants to talk to you."

"Tell him to come on back," Meade said and waited, his cigar clenched firmly between his teeth. A moment later, Reilly came through the arch, a spare man in his middle twenties.

"Murray's outside," Reilly said. "He wants to see you right away, Meade."

"In a minute," Meade told him.

"He won't wait," Reilly said.

"Tell him not to be a damn fool and come in here," Meade said evenly. "I'll be out."

"I'll tell him," Reilly said and jerked his thumb toward the street. "Clymer and Garroway are standin' out there like they was guardin' the hen-house. They going to keep out of this?"

"It depends on what you and Sam do," Meade said and glanced at the walnut-handled .45 that Reilly was never without. "Butt in, Reilly, and you're liable to run into something solid."

"This is between you and Murray," Reilly said. "Maybe I wish it was going to be different, but Murray's a hard fella to convince when he lays his ears down."

"That makes two of us," Meade said and watched the man leave. Rising from the table, Meade threw away his cigar and picked up his hat.

Amy said, "You won't kill him, Meade. Killing isn't in you."

"You know me that well?"

She didn't answer, so he opened the back door and stepped into the alley. He moved down the littered darkness until he came to the end of it,

73

then turned left and paused when he came to the corner of Lode. There were no shop lights here, so he crossed over, using darkness to cover him.

He found the other alley entrance and moved through it until he came to the back of the hotel. He let himself in, came to the lobby, and crossed it. Allene Gruen was behind the desk, surprised to see him on this side of the street.

Meade stepped through the front door of the hotel, then moved to the right of the entrance, where the shadows were heaviest, and waited. He remembered the sound of Amy's voice, and he did not deny that she spoke the truth. Faced with it, he was not up to killing Murray Sinclair, for he felt no hatred toward the man. Murray was a fighter who asked no quarter and gave none.

Up to this point, he had thought he knew Murray well, but now he was no longer sure and he felt the first frost of fear. There was nothing predictable about a man on the near edge of killing. All rules were cast aside, and new patterns of behavior asserted themselves.

Lode Street was vacant, except for Clymer and Garroway standing in the shadows by the mercantile wall. A little farther down, Sam and Reilly Sinclair waited, outlined by a small shard of reflected light from a shop window.

Stepping to the edge of the street, Meade turned his head slowly from side to side, like a dog sniffing scent. When he picked up the high shape of Murray Sinclair standing in a darkened doorway, it was more an instinctive awareness than an actual sighting of the man.

Bigelow was at a disadvantage, but the hurried habits of a lifetime tripped Murray, and he drew too fast, shot too quickly. The bullet touched Meade high on the thigh, left a shallow, burning groove in the muscle, and whined on.

Dipping a hand beneath his coat, Meade palmed the .44 as Murray shot again, driving a shower of dust over Bigelow's boots. As Meade brought the gun up, Murray left the darkened doorway, and Meade shot carefully, once, feeling the recoil shock his palm.

Murray reacted like a puppet on a string. The gun flew from his hand, and he was jerked back against a glass window, bringing it down with him as he collapsed.

People charged from the doorways then, and Meade slipped his gun back into the spring holster beneath his armpit. Across the street, Sam and Reilly vacated the shelter of the building, but stopped when Clymer said, "That's far enough with guns! Drop the cartridge belts first, then go to him."

For a moment, Meade thought that Clymer had invited a fight, but the two brothers let their gun belts plop into the dust and broke into a run.

Trying to sit up, Murray was pawing at the blood seeping from his side. Meade's bullet had caught him just above the belt and had torn through the fleshy part, missing the vital organs but knocking the wind out of him.

Hoisted by Sam and Reilly, Murray raised his head and stared at Meade Bigelow. "You should have finished the job, Mr. Great Northern."

"Better get some sense, Murray," Meade said. "You can't buck the world and win." He crossed to the arcade post and leaned, for his legs felt weak and blood made a warm ooze down his calf.

Jim Hardesty came up on a run, his swivel holster flopping wildly. He looked at Murray for a moment, then turned to Meade. Barnum and Allendale pushed their way through the crowd, Amy Falcon following in their wake. The lamplight streaming from the hotel made the blood on Bigelow's leg almost black.

Amy saw it and said, "Meade," but he looked at her and shook his head, and she fell silent.

Bigelow was amazed how fast a crowd could gather, for they were three deep around them now, and thickening. Jim Hardesty began to attack the crowd with his elbows and sharp voice. When he had cleared an avenue, he said, "Sam, Reilly—get him through here and to the doctor."

They half-carried Murray, and Reilly turned his head toward Bigelow. "You want a goddam war, Meade—we'll give you one you won't live through."

"Talk's cheap," Meade said flatly. "Get out of the country and don't waste any time doing it."

Clymer and Garroway had edged unnoticed into the crowd, and when Reilly released his brother and took a step toward Meade, Clymer raised the muzzle of his .44 Evans and said, "Uh, uh, Reilly. I shoot to kill."

"Get him out of here," Hardesty ordered, and Reilly turned away from Clymer. The crowd began to lose interest rapidly and broke away in chattering fragments.

Hardesty waited until they had dispersed, then turned to Meade. "I don't like to have Great Northern make the law in my town, Meade. I told you that once before."

"Well now," Meade said and straightened away from the post. He reached out and hooked his fingers around Hardesty's badge, then ripped it from the man's coat. "Great Northern just fired you. We'll pay you to the end of the month."

For a moment Hardesty swayed on the edge of violence and his cheeks paled beneath his tan. "So that's how it is," he murmured. "Great Northern controls the votes, too." He looked across the street to Reilly and Sam who carried Murray up the stairs leading to Dr. Walker's office over the saddlemaker's. "I think you just made your first big mistake, Meade." He smiled then, but the frostiness never left his eyes. "You're a big man, Meade, but there are some angles that you don't know. I'll have that badge back on inside of an hour."

"You think so?" Meade asked.

"Stick around and see," Hardesty said and brushed past Bigelow, ramming him heavily with his shoulder.

Meade's legs began to tremble, and a deep burning commenced where Murray's bullet had nicked him. Amy Falcon took his arm and said, "I was wrong, Meade—you should have killed him. It will be war now."

"I think you're right," he said and spent a moment lighting a cigar.

"Let me fix your leg," she said. "Is it bad?"

"I don't think so," he murmured and looked up and down the street. "I should go see Conover."

"It can wait," she said and took his arm. He began to limp badly when they turned the corner, walked a block to a side street, then followed it to the end. Amy Falcon's home was little more than a small cabin sitting at the end of a tree-covered lane.

She opened the door and went in ahead of him to light the lamp. After he sat down, she built a small fire in the stove and put on a pan of water to heat.

Taking a sharp knife from the table drawer, she said, "Slit open the seam so that I can sew it up again."

He was glad of the chance to sit down and

settled himself on the straw-filled tick. There wasn't much to the cabin, just a rough room with the barest of furniture.

"There's a blanket to wrap yourself in while I mend the pants," she said and turned her back to him while he undressed.

"First the supper, then alone in your cabin," Meade said. "I don't think either of us is going to have much of a reputation after tonight."

"Who cares?" she said and took the water off the stove.

Chapter Six

At seven o'clock the professor at Karen's Saloon had his breakfast of bourbon and brown beans at the free-lunch counter and sat down to the piano to limber his fingers. On a back street the Odd Fellows hall sported lamplight in the windows and hanging *papier-mâché* lanterns, and old Charlie Bourne moved around the dance floor, scattering flaked wax while a five-piece string band tuned up in the corner.

In Heavy Pearl's darkened and anonymous house, Jean and Millie sat listlessly over their coffee cups, and the night grew older and more alive as Lode Street began to fill with shouting men.

Jim Hardesty went to the hotel after the fight. On his face the anger that had churned so hotly died, and when he reached the head of the stairs to pause before Allene Gruen's door, his face held only a determination to put Meade Bigelow in his place.

Allene opened the door, and he stepped inside, tossing his hat onto a chair. She wore a light-blue dressing gown of nearly transparent material, and when she walked it whispered invitingly.

She said, "You let him make a fool of you, Jim. I don't like it."

He moved close to her and put his arm around

the softness of her waist. "What could I do? When Meade starts a thing, it's hard to take it away from him until he's finished with it."

She pushed his hands away. "You're being paid to take care of these things," she said. "Jim, Dan Conover is not going to like this at all."

He slapped his thigh, half angry again. "Dammit, I was told to handle it lightly. I ask you, what was I to do?" He put his hands on her shoulders and turned her to face him. "Allie," he said softly and pulled her against him. "Let's not quarrel over this, Allie."

He kissed her, and her arms went around his neck tightly, then her palms were against his chest and she freed herself. "Damn you, Jim! Once you find a woman's weakness, you play it to the hilt, don't you?"

"I thought we loved each other," he said and watched her carefully.

"Love?" She said it like a child experimenting with a new word. "I tried that once, Jim, and it wasn't enough. You know what I mean, but I can't help myself."

"It's all right," he said. "That's enough for me."

"Sometimes I wonder," she murmured and picked up his hat, holding it out to him. "You'd better see Dan Conover right away. He'll know what to do now."

"You're right," he said and tried to kiss her again, but she fended him off.

"When the town quiets down," she said, and a slight smile lifted the ends of her full lips. "Later, Jim—you know."

He went out then and heard the lock snap as he closed the door. Leaving the hotel, Jim Hardesty turned toward the far end of the street and walked rapidly. At the corner he turned toward the residential district and Dan Conover's house.

The colored woman let him in and ushered him into Conover's book-lined study, closing the door after him. Conover was behind his desk, going over a financial statement with Cord Butram, chief clerk for Great Northern.

Raising his eyes at this intrusion, Conover said, "Will you excuse us for a moment, Cord. Hattie will fix you a drink."

Butram uncoiled his length from the chair and went out after giving Hardesty a pale smile. He was a balding man and wore rimless glasses perched on the high arch of his nose. His shoulders were slightly rounded and the seat of his dark suit was highly polished.

When the study door closed again, Conover speared Hardesty with his dark eyes, and the little man's beard seemed to bristle.

"So Meade Bigelow took away your badge?"

Hardesty shifted his feet and looked uncertain. "What did you want me to do, wrestle him on the street?" He made a disgusted motion. "Your orders were none too clear, if you want to know it. That was a damn thin fence you wanted me to straddle."

"I told you I didn't want Murray hurt," Conover said and slapped his desk. He spent a minute lighting a cigar, then added, "Damn, how could I have misjudged Meade like that? I never figured he'd shoot a man—it just didn't seem to fit."

"I'm thinkin' you made a mistake," Hardesty murmured, feeling that he was on safer ground now.

"I've made several of them," Conover said. "Hardesty, I'm going to make Meade's firing you stick. Your pay will go on, but we'll have to get someone else to carry the badge." He raised his hand when Hardesty tried to speak. "I'm not going to argue with you, Jim. I'll just have to get someone else for the job."

"I think I'm being pushed out," Hardesty murmured. He leaned forward, placing his palms flat on Dan Conover's desk. "I ran this town the way you wanted it, but now you're not satisfied. You told me to keep Murray Sinclair out of trouble, but you never said how far to go. If I had used my own judgment and gone too far, you'd have raised hell. Now you're raising hell because I didn't go far enough." His eyebrows pulled down into a troubled line. "What kind of game are you playing here? What's the connection? I either know or you can stick your job."

"I'll have Cord Butram pay you to the end of

the month," Conover said flatly and puffed on his cigar. "You're the kind of man who doesn't know his place, Hardesty. Get your hands off my desk!"

Hardesty straightened slowly, and in his eyes a hard light burned. "All right," he said. "You play your close game, Dan, but somebody is going to call your bluff."

"It won't be you," Conover said. "Now get out. I'm a busy man."

Cord Butram was in the parlor, talking to June in a soft voice when Hardesty went out. Butram set his drink aside, excused himself, and went back in Conover's study.

Conover was pacing back and forth, a cloud of cigar smoke trying to follow him. Butram took a chair by the large desk and crossed his abnormally long legs. Finally Conover stopped pacing.

"Cord, pay Hardesty to the end of the month and tell Clymer to get him out of town."

"Right away?"

"Tonight," Conover said. "I no longer trust the man."

"He's only hired help," Butram murmured.

"That's right," Conover agreed, "but the man is smart and he's curious. That can be a bad combination." He paused to relieve the cigar ash. "See if you can find Meade Bigelow. I want to see him right away."

"All right," Butram said and stood up. "Shall I tell Clymer?"

"Yes," Conover said and dropped his attention to some papers on his desk, dismissing Butram.

The wound in Meade Bigelow's thigh was neither deep nor serious, and after washing it, Amy placed a moist bandage on it and pronounced it cured. In the privacy of his folded blanket, Meade waited while she washed the blood from his pants and dried them over the stove.

He sat by the table, a blanket wrapped around his hips. His thigh ached with a steady, monotonous throbbing, and he tried to put his mind away from it by concentrating on Amy sewing the seam and bullet tear in the pant leg.

Lamplight was kind to her, for her skin held the last of a summer's deep tan, contrasting sharply with her gold-colored hair. Her eyelashes were long against her cheeks, and her full lips quietly reposed.

Occasionally she looked up from her sewing and watched him, even as he watched her. "You look funny in that blanket," she said and laughed. "I've always wondered what a man would look like in a skirt, and now I know."

"I feel silly," Meade told her. He touched a match to his cigar and puffed slowly, watching the smoke rise to the log rafters and flatten against the ceiling. He felt perfectly at ease with her and decided that it was her frank manner that made him feel this way. He would never have to pretend around this woman, for she knew him well beyond the veil of pretense.

"Here's your pants, Pocahontas," Amy said and left the table. She turned her back to him while he dressed, and he had some difficulty with his right leg.

"You can turn around now," he said, tucking in his shirt tail.

"Care for some coffee now?"

"Fine," he said and limped over to the stove to get rid of his cigar.

Knuckles rattled against the front door, and Amy shot him a questioning glance. She moved around Meade and opened it quickly. Cord Butram swept off his hat and said, "Sorry to intrude, but is Meade Bigelow here? A fellow on the street said he saw him walking toward your house after the shooting."

"Come in," Amy said and closed the door.

"How are you, Meade? You got away so fast no one was sure how bad you were hit."

"Just a scratch," Meade said. "Sit down, Cord, and have some coffee."

"Thanks, but some other time." Butram's face was smooth and earnest. "Mr. Conover wants to see you, Meade. Right away, he said."

"In a few minutes," Meade murmured. "Sure you won't have some coffee, Cord?"

"Thanks, no," Butram said and moved toward the door. "I have work to do." He nodded pleasantly to Amy and stepped out.

Meade said, "I guess I'd better go, Amy." He put on his coat.

"Are you coming back?"

He shook his head. "It wouldn't be wise," he said. "We're renegades, you and I. Too headstrong for our own good."

"Take care of yourself," she said softly. "Reilly and Sam might still be around."

"I'll watch," he murmured and touched her arm. "Thanks for everything, Amy." He dropped his hand and left the small cabin, walking carefully down the darkened path leading to the back street.

Hardesty paused on the boardwalk at the end of Lode Street, filled with the driving anger that comes to a man who is blamed for something that he does not know anything about. Walking again, he threaded his way through the crowd moving up and down the street and crossed over to Karen's Saloon.

Once inside, he found a place at the crowded bar and ordered a drink when Lonigan paused before him. Sweat ran down the bartender's face, and he moved with feverish haste.

The room was thick with the sound of men's voices, and over in the west corner, the professor tried to drown it out with a lively tune.

Hardesty sagged against the bar, returning a few greetings but keeping to himself. An hour went by slowly, for he was not accustomed to idleness, and his mind kept leaving and making the rounds that habit had set up for him.

After the second drink, the anger began to dissolve and he began to form plans for the future. With no job and none around here that he wanted, he could move on, but then he thought of Allene Gruen and thoughts of moving faded.

From long habit, he kept one eye on the door, and he saw Clymer come in and move directly to the other end of the bar. The man elbowed his way to the cherrywood and brushed two men's drinks aside with the barrel of his repeating rifle.

After taking his drink in one toss of the head, Clymer turned slightly and nodded to Jim Hardesty. Through the hubbub of noise along the bar, Clymer's voice rose, and men turned their heads toward him.

"You see the way Great Northern handled that wise marshal?" He laughed in a booming voice and shot Hardesty a sly glance.

The men on each side of Clymer grew quiet and very attentive. He looked around to see how big his audience was, and went on. "I never seen anything like it. Bigelow just reached out and took it off his coat, like a kid taking candy.

Hardesty's knees was shakin' so damn bad he could hardly walk away."

There was a stunned moment of silence along the bar, and then Hardesty reached out and knocked a whisky bottle to the floor, where it broke with a sharp crash.

Voices died quickly, and the professor concluded his number in the middle of a bar and turned on his stool to see what was the cause of this silence.

When Hardesty stepped away from the angle of the bar and moved a few steps toward Clymer, men hurriedly got out of the way. Twenty feet separated these two men, and Hardesty said, "You're in a mouthy mood tonight, Clymer. Something on your mind?"

"I was just wondering," Clymer said, "if it would be any fun to chase you up a tree tonight."

"Don't try it," Hardesty said softly. "Don't try anything."

Clymer laughed and laid a hand on his .44 Evans. "I don't think there's any fight in you, Hardesty—just bark."

"Be careful now," Hardesty said. He had his thumb hooked in his belt, and the swivel holster was no more than four inches from his hand.

Clymer's hand curled around the stock of his rifle, and a thin smile caused crow's-feet to appear around his eyes. There was no sound in the room save the sawing of men's breathing.

Clymer's rifle lay flat on the bar, the muzzle pointing in Hardesty's direction.

For a full minute the two men stood there; then Clymer laughed and swept the Evans clear of the polished top. Hardesty's hand dropped, and gun and holster pivoted on a rivet. A large blossom of fire erupted from the muzzle, and the detonation rattled bottles and glasses behind the bar.

Clymer was slammed back and whirled half around. His uptilted rifle went off, plowing a sliver from the ceiling, and then he fell awkwardly, his head rapping the brass footrail as he slumped to the floor.

Hardesty stood there for a moment, his gun still pointed at the spot where the dead man had stood; then his hand dropped away, and the gun pivoted, swinging back and forth on the rivet in decreasing arcs.

Felix Karen came from the back room, a big man dressed in a fine suit and flowered vest. He glanced at Clymer and then at Hardesty. "What was it all about, Jim?"

"I don't know," Hardesty admitted. "I just don't know." He took a long breath and pushed past the row of men who stood unmoving. At the front door, he turned and looked back at Clymer, then went out, and the noise began to build up again, swelling to a roar as each man tried to talk at once.

Walking along the quiet back street toward Dan Conover's house, Meade Bigelow heard the near, blending shots from Lode, but the sound was not new or unusual to him and he thought no more of it.

The colored woman let him in, took his hat, and ushered him directly to Dan Conover's study. June was in the living room, and she stood up as Meade appeared briefly in the archway, but he shook his head and followed Hattie.

Conover and Cord Butram were at the desk, and Butram excused himself as Meade entered. Waiting until the door was closed, Conover said, "Meade, I don't know exactly what to say to you."

"Start from the top," Bigelow said. "That's as good a way as any I know."

"All right," Conover said and walked back and forth, his bearded chin outthrust, his hands clasped behind his back. "Meade, I'm afraid that you've bungled things inexcusably."

"You'll have to explain that," Meade said, and his brows drew together.

Conover stopped pacing and went behind his desk to his soft swivel chair. "Meade, Great Northern's position in regard to the Sinclairs is a very delicate one. Their mine is rich and would yield a nice profit, if they could be persuaded to enter a cartel relationship."

"I understand that," Meade said. "Frankly, sir, I don't get your point."

"My point," Conover said, "is that instead of reaching a sound business agreement with Murray Sinclair, you allowed yourself to be chivvied into gunplay. I expected better than that out of you, Meade!"

"Now wait a minute," Meade said. "Several times you gave me permission to handle this in my own way, and I did. Now you're telling me that I didn't handle it like you wanted. Why the hell didn't you say what you wanted in the first place?"

For a minute, Conover stared at Meade Bigelow, a deep anger in his eyes. "Your tone is on the borderline of being inexcusable, but for the moment I will overlook it. Listen to me, Meade, and understand this once and for all. You are the general superintendent of Great Northern, but you do not make company policy nor over-extend your authority such as you did today."

"Now see here—"

"Kindly wait until I am finished," Conover said. "You have ruined, I believe, our chances of bringing Murray Sinclair up on the rope by causing him to be openly antagonistic to cartelized interests."

"Murray shot a man," Meade said tightly. "You saw Garvey's sworn statement!"

Conover waved this aside. "Men have made

mistakes in identity before, Meade. It could have happened this time. Had you used your head toward the last and refused Murray's fight, as I had hoped you would, Jim Hardesty could have arrested the man and charges could have been brought against him. If he had come to his senses and joined the cartel with his mine, the charges could have been dismissed and Garvey's statement refuted." Conover's lips were thin. "Meade, you have bungled a very important assignment."

"So *I've* bungled it?" Meade asked softly. "Mr. Conover, did Murray kill Goofy Harris?"

Conover moved his hands aimlessly. "Who can definitely say? All that matters is that I had Murray worked into a position where he was going to jail, and you took him off the hook with a gunfight." Conover pounded the desk with his fist. "You didn't have the goddam guts to kill him while you were at it and save it that way!"

Beneath Meade's mustache his lips were drawn and white. A hot anger danced in his eyes, but none of this showed in his voice. "I've been hearing a lot of talk about Great Northern, and I've taken great care not to lose my temper and tell people off. But right now I don't give a damn. It seems to me that you have something up your sleeve and I'm in the dark. Well, you can just keep it that way."

"What do you mean?" Conover asked.

"For three years I've worked my butt raw building Great Northern both in size and production. I've worked too damned hard to have my head snapped off by you or anyone else." Bigelow leaned on Conover's desk, his face a foot from the old man's cigar. "Get yourself another boy, Dan—I'm quitting, as of now."

"Why—why, you're acting hastily now," Conover sputtered. "Tomorrow you'll feel differently."

"No I won't," Meade said. "Let me tell you something, Dan. You've got a big machine here, and you've shoved it down people's throats and made them like it. But the truth is, they don't like it. They want it busted up. Murray wants it that way, and a lot of others are behind him.

"I've done my job and squeezed people when I didn't want to do it, because I'm a Great Northern man. Now I'm not and I can tell you what I think. I didn't want to push Murray tonight. I wanted to shoot him even less, but whether you believe it or not, he had Great Northern in a position where talk was no good."

"Get out of my office!" Conover snapped. "Go on—get out!"

"My pleasure," Bigelow said and walked to the door as it opened suddenly. Cord Butram looked excited, and he breathed heavily as though he had been in a hurry to get back.

Butram glanced at Meade, then said, "Mr.

Conover—Jim Hardesty just killed Clymer!"

"What?" Conover was up on his feet, poised as though he were preparing to leap over the desk.

From the expression of unbelief on Conover's face, Meade read a great deal. His laugh was soft and mocking. "So you sicked that killer on Hardesty, but Jim turned out to be a better man. Did Garvey pull the trigger on Goofy Harris, too?"

Impulsively, Conover gripped a heavy inkwell and raised it. Bigelow's smile widened, and he closed the door behind him.

When he turned down the hall to leave, he found June standing in the archway, her hands clasped together, a definite worry in her eyes. Meade knew that she had heard the conversation.

Chapter Seven

For a moment neither spoke; then June came forward and took his arm. "Darling," she said, "you're angry. Come and sit down."

"Haven't I a right to be?" His voice was brittle, but when he spoke again, it was in a softer tone. "Sorry, June. I have no right to take it out on you."

"I understand," she said and took him into the parlor. She closed the large double doors, poured him a drink, and then sat down by his feet. "Please, Meade. Try to understand Father. He's upset."

"I'm upset," Bigelow said and tossed the brandy off. "June, what went wrong tonight? I played the game for Great Northern, right down the line, but somehow it didn't satisfy your father. He wants it different."

"Please," June said, "forget about it, darling. Tomorrow you two will apologize and shake hands, and it might never have happened for all you'll think about it." She put her hand on his knee and shook him gently until he looked at her. "Meade, you didn't mean what you said about quitting, did you?"

"I meant it," he said. "He knows I meant it."

She smiled and spread her hands. "Meade, it's

so silly, really. You're a brilliant man, an engineer. You can't throw that away just because you lost your temper."

"June," he said seriously and leaned forward, "this kind of thing builds up in a man for a long time, then it boils over. A man in my position hears a lot of talk, and most of it is against Great Northern. Most of it I pass off as coming from cranks who're sore because they don't collect on the jackpot, but when Marilee Hart and Buckley, not to mention Barnum and Allendale, speak out openly against Great Northern, then something is wrong."

"That's ridiculous!" June snapped. "Meade, these little people are always crying because there's something they don't like. I thought you of all people would see through them."

"What's there to see through?" he asked. He shook his head. "I don't know what's going on anymore. I know that Murray would like to see Great Northern's power split up again and I know that your father is fighting him, but right now I'm not so sure the fight is clean."

"Clean?" June said. "Meade, with what's at stake, who can help hitting below the belt?"

"Do you think Murray is?" He waited for her answer, and when she didn't speak, added, "He's hot-headed and tough, but I've never heard anything mean about him. That's why I held off as long as I did about the silver robberies. Honey, I just wasn't sure that Murray did it. I wasn't sure when I shot him in the side. If I had been, he'd be dead now."

"And now you think my father is trying to implicate Murray, is that it?"

"Since you put it into words—yes."

She bit her lower lip, and there was a hint of tears in her eyes. "Meade, I love you and I want to marry you. Do you believe that?"

"Yes," he said. "It worried me some—how you would feel."

"I'll never feel differently toward you," she said and put her arms around him, pillowing her head against his chest. She held him for a long moment, then backed away a step. "How is your leg, Meade? Forgive me for not asking."

"It will be all right," he murmured.

"Was Murray at the doctor's office when you were there?"

"I didn't go to the doctor," he said and saw the large question in her eyes. "Amy Falcon patched me up."

Into June's eyes there came a complete understanding, and her voice was like a cool wind. "How convenient that must have been—for both of you."

"You're not jealous, are you?"

"Jealous?" She tipped her head back and laughed. "Meade, you have the strangest sense of humor. I'll have to thank her for taking such good care of you."

He studied her face for a moment and shrewdly guessed that further talk was useless. Taking his hat, he limped to the sliding doors and pulled them open, halting when she ran up to him and threw her arms around him.

"I am jealous," she said and kissed him fervently. "Meade, let's not go wrong with each other. You will be back, won't you?"

"Not here," he said. "We'll see each other, June. Somehow we'll manage." He kissed her again and let himself out.

Moving through the darkness to Lode, he wondered why he had acted so hastily, and decided that the line between right and wrong was so fine that a man had only the dictates of his conscience to guide him at times.

Traffic was still thick on the street, and he stood on the corner for ten minutes, trying to find the tall shape of Jim Hardesty. When he failed to see the man, he turned again toward the back street and navigated the lane leading to Amy Falcon's cabin.

Through the curtained window he saw a shard of light escaping along the bottom and rapped on the door. Her answering footsteps came to him, muffled; then the door opened, and she smiled when she recognized him.

"You're just in time for a party," Amy said, and

when Meade glanced past her, he saw Marilee Hart and Jules Buckley seated at the table. Jim Hardesty leaned against the log wall, his face grave.

"Quite a gathering," Meade said and tossed his hat on Amy's bed. "I think I'm elected to this *élite* group—I just quit Great Northern."

Amy was taking cups down from the cupboard, and she released one, letting it splinter against the floor. Jules Buckley's eyes came up to Meade's face and held. On Marilee's face there was a look of shocked surprise, and Jim Hardesty shifted his feet; there was no sound in the room.

"Why?" Buckley asked. "You had a lot to give up, Meade."

Amy bent to retrieve the broken cup, and some of the tension fled from the room. She set dishes on the table and poured from a blackened coffee-pot. Because there were no more chairs, Meade sat on the edge of Amy's bed. She came over and sat beside him.

Meade said, "Conover, I think, tried to pin something on Murray that Murray didn't do."

"Explain that," Marilee said. "Excuse us, Meade, but you've been Mr. Big for a long time. A thing like this takes some time to get used to."

Meade sipped his coffee, then explained Conover's anger because he had shot Murray. "I don't fully understand it," Meade said, "but I'm sure that Conover wanted Murray safe and sound

100

for some reason or another. I came too close to killing something important and it made him mad—and scared."

Hardesty stirred from his position along the wall. "Clymer was primed to kill me tonight. Meade, I want to know—did Dan sick him on me?"

"I think so," Meade said, and Hardesty nodded.

Marilee Hart looked at Jules Buckley and said, "Meade, Murray Sinclair did not hold up the silver shipment. Neither did Sam or Reilly. They were sleeping soundly in the cookshack at the cutting mill the night it happened. Thirty of my men will swear to it."

"Why didn't you tell me this before, Marilee?" Meade asked.

"Would you have believed me?"

Meade scrubbed a hand across his face. "I guess not, but I sure do now." He switched his eyes from one to the other. "What's Dan Conover up to?"

"I don't know," Buckley murmured. "We were thinking about that before you came in. Maybe you can tell us, Meade. You know all about this high finance."

"I think he's trying to corner Great Northern for himself," Jim Hardesty said.

Meade shook his head. "I don't think so, Jim. He started out with thirty per cent of Silver City Land and Trust, so of course he gets the hog's share of the profits all the way around, but the voting shares are held by a lot of little people with five and ten dollars. He'd have to buy up their stock, and that would break him, since Great Northern stock is up now. He'd have to spend two dollars and a half to get one dollar's worth of goods. No, there must be something else."

Jules Buckley slapped his leg and stood up, stretching. He put his hand on Marilee's shoulder and said, "Thanks for the coffee, Amy, but we have a long drive ahead of us." Marilee vacated her chair, and they moved across the room. At the door she turned to Meade.

"Jules won't ask you, but I will. What are you going to do now?"

"I haven't thought about it," Meade said.

"Why don't you have a talk with Murray Sinclair?"

He shook his head. "I shot him tonight, remember? I don't want to have anything to do with Great Northern—for or against."

"I see," Marilee said and went out with Jules Buckley.

Finished with his cup, Jim Hardesty took it to the wooden sink and rinsed it. He took his hat from a wall peg, then whirled it in his hands for a moment. "Meade, be careful with yourself now. This puts you in the same canoe as I'm in, and Clymer wasn't the last of Great Northern's toughs."

"I'll keep it in mind," Meade said and stared at the door after Hardesty went out.

The sounds of the town filtered through the walls, and water from the pump plunger dripped quietly in the sink. Amy swirled the coffee grounds around in the bottom of her cup, then got up and gathered the dishes.

Meade still sat on the edge of her bed, his back hunched, staring at the pattern of knots on the bare floor. "This turned out to be a hell of a night," he said. "Why was Clymer after Jim? Did he say?"

"He doesn't know," Amy murmured. "Conover fired him and told him to get out of town. Clymer made his try an hour later."

"A man's not gunned for nothing," Meade murmured. He stood up and walked across the room to where she worked at the sink. Touching her gently on the arm, he said, "Let's go over to the Odd Fellows hall and listen to the music."

"I'll get my wrap," Amy said and dried her hands. She whirled a shawl around her shoulders, and Meade held the door open for her. Amy paused to snuff out the lamps, and then Meade closed the door and they walked off into the night.

There was a cool wind blowing, and it carried the music along, wavering and muted by distance. The noise of Lode Street seemed far away, and they walked slowly, with Meade favoring his sore leg.

They cut across another darkened street and followed a lane that led to the rear of the hall. As they drew nearer, the sound of laughter wafted out on the wind and the musicians played with a frantic beat.

The three-block walk gave Meade more trouble than he had anticipated, and when they neared the tree-dotted yard, he said, "I guess I'm too big for my pants, Amy, but I just got to sit down. You go on in and dance while I take life easy with a cigar."

"We'll both sit under the trees," she said and squatted in the grass. The hall was twenty yards away, and lamplight streamed from the windows in golden torrents. She straightened her legs, and the outline was long and tapered beneath her cotton dress.

Men came out and laughingly passed the jug, then went back inside to come out again a few minutes later. For a while they sat there, listening to the blended sounds of people having a good time. Amy said, "The tougher life is, the harder they laugh and dance to forget it."

He selected a cigar from his shirt pocket and arced a match. "Is life that tough, Amy?"

Her shoulders rose and fell, and when he settled back against the tree he could feel the warmth of her when they touched. "No one makes money in Silver City, Meade. Not even Felix Karen at the saloon." She lifted her skirts to the knee, exposing legs that were rounded and smooth. She crossed one over the other and took off her shoes and set them side by side. She rubbed her feet in the grass and said, "See, too poor to wear socks."

She stood up suddenly and took his arm. "There's a creek back there." She pointed to an alder-studded thicket in back of the hall. "I'd like to go wading."

Lamplight touched her face, revealing a mischievous sparkle in her eyes. Meade stood up and said, "Eternal youth."

Skirting the hall, they moved through the grass that grew higher than their knees. There was some timber here, aspen and scrub oak. Amy paused to tie up her skirts, and then clutching her shoes, ran to catch up with Meade.

The creek wiggled a crooked path a hundred yards behind the hall, gurgling like an infant in delight. Bigelow found a place beneath a gnarled tree where moss grew thick and clear water lapped at the exposed roots.

Sinking down, Amy dropped her skirt around her ankles and sat with her feet tucked under her. Night sounds were all around them. Frogs sang an off-key chorus, and small animals rustled the grass in search of food.

A sliver of a moon passed overhead, and a few stars braved the darkness. Occasionally sheetlike clouds floated past, thin as transparent cloth.

Meade said, "I told June that you patched me up. She wasn't too delighted."

"I'm sorry," Amy murmured. "I didn't want you to quarrel over it."

"It doesn't matter," he said softly. "People will always find something to bicker about."

"Is she right for you, Meade?"

"I think so," he murmured. "She's cultured, and she meets people well. Maybe I don't feel all flame and violence inside when I'm with her, but there's enough there to last."

"A man would think like that," she said. "But a woman is different." She leaned back on stiffened arms, her breasts thrust out against the bodice of her dress. "I like the smells here. If you try and sniff easy, you can pick them out, Indian paintbrush, ragweed, some sage." She looked at Meade and laughed. "Back home in Texas I used to sit and smell the air. Did I ever tell you about my home, Meade?"

"No, you never did."

"I had eight brothers and sisters," Amy said. She rolled over and rested on her elbows. "When I get married and have daughters, I'm going to build each of them a cabin when they're eighteen. When a girl grows up, her mother ceases to look on her as a daughter. Instead she sees her as a marriageable female, the sooner rid of, the better."

"What brought you to Silver City, Amy? The lure of riches?"

"They're not for me," Amy murmured. "No, I think I just wanted to be free." She fell silent for a moment. "How did you feel when you proposed to June? Were you nervous?"

Meade laughed softly. "To tell you the truth, I didn't. We just drifted into an understanding. I met her when Conover hired me. She was witty and charming, and I guess that's what I admired in her. Looking back on it, I think we understood how it was going to be from the very beginning."

"That doesn't sound too romantic," Amy said frankly. "The man I marry is going to have to drag me off by the hair."

"You're joking!" Meade said in a surprised voice.

"I was never more serious in my life," Amy told him. "Do you think I want the kind of man who comes to the door with flowers and smelling of hair tonic? If he wants me, he'd better kick the door down, grab me, and tell me that he's crazy about me. Then if I'm stupid enough to argue with a man like that, he should throw me over his shoulder and pack me off."

"That," Meade said, "is an entirely new approach." He settled back, his hands behind his head. "I'll have to investigate the possibilities of that sometime."

"You think too much," Amy said. "I'm stupid and happy, simply because I didn't finish the sixth grade."

"Sixth grade for me was a long time ago," Meade said. "We lived in a white house with a bronze deer on the lawn. Father was county surveyor who married in his second year and couldn't finish college and keep a wife at the same time." He punched the ash from his dead cigar with his forefinger and paused to light it. "The only way I could get an education was West Point, so I took it. After my tour, I resigned to take another year of engineering."

"You're a strange man," Amy said. "A mixture of solemn sage and impulsive boy. You ought to obey your impulses more often, Meade."

"I'd land in jail. Look what I did tonight."

"Impulsiveness is akin to honesty," she said. "You agree, don't you?"

"In an abstract way," he said, "I suppose I do, but I'm honest and yet I've spent most of my life learning to control my impulses."

"Then you're honest with others and not yourself," Amy said. "You shouldn't cheat yourself like that, Meade. It's not fair."

Immediately he understood that she had touched on a great truth about him, and with this understanding, he could see where many things in his life would have been drastically altered had he acted by instinct instead of clinging to his methodical ways.

"Let's see about impulses," Meade said and turned over, pulling her against him.

He meant it to be a gentle kiss, one of restraint to show that he was only teasing her, but reaction mauled him like a fist at the base of the skull.

In the touch of her lips there were his dreams, his hopes, his longings, and the sudden discovery shocked him immeasurably. Her arms around his neck were warm, holding him possessively but not restricting him. He was amazed that his mind could remain so objective while her lips seared him.

The kiss lasted much longer than he had intended, for once started, it was something over which he had little control. Even after they parted, the memory remained strong and undimmed for him.

She lay back and stared at the night sky. He found his cigar again and began to light it, then changed his mind and whipped out the match.

"That was a stupid, thoughtless thing for me to do, wasn't it?"

"Was it, Meade?" Her voice was barely a whisper.

"I'll take you back," he said and stood up, pulling her to her feet. For an instant they touched when she swayed against him, and he had to exert all his will to beat down the impulse to kiss her again.

She bent to pick up her shoes and slipped into them, and when she took his hand, said nothing as they walked back toward her cabin.

Meade did not want to compare her to June Conover, but that was something over which he had little control. Somehow, when June put her arms around him, she left him with the feeling that she was binding him, although she always caressed him lightly. Always she seemed to be withholding a part of her affection, never giving herself completely. These were things he had never noticed before, because he had never known a woman to surrender herself completely as Amy Falcon had.

To Meade's way of thinking, his woman would have to be gentle and not too demanding on his life, but now he wondered whether he could ever be satisfied by half measures. How was he to measure a woman's worth? What was the scale a man used? Instinct? That seemed too sketchy and untrustworthy, and he discarded the idea.

Arriving at the cabin, Meade stopped by the doorway and touched Amy Falcon on the arm. "Good night," he said softly and wanted to say a lot more, but he couldn't unravel the tangle of his emotions enough to speak.

"Good night, Meade," Amy said and wouldn't look at him. He touched her under the chin to bring her face around, but she shook her head and murmured, "Please don't, Meade."

She went in and closed the door, and he stared at it for a moment before turning to go down the darkened path. At the mouth, he stopped, for he had heard a sound. He raised his hand to his coat and unbuttoned it, then halted all motion as Reilly Sinclair said, "Don't move, Meade! There's two guns on your back."

Chapter Eight

Meade Bigelow pressed both palms flat against his chest, and Sam Sinclair came out of the brush to his left, flipped the lapel of Meade's coat aside, and ripped the short-barreled .44 from the shoulder holster.

Reilly stepped out then, his long-barreled .45 in his hand. "Don't give us any trouble, Meade," Reilly murmured.

"I'll give you plenty of trouble," Meade said, but stood very still. Sam tucked Meade's gun in the waistband of his pants and stepped back.

"We'll take the back street now," Reilly said softly. "Try anything and we'll bend you out of shape. You understand?"

"I understand," Meade said and followed Sam.

They skirted Silver City, walked the length of a back street, then turned into a dark lane. Meade limped badly, and Sam slowed his pace. Houses were scattered in this neighborhood, and finally Reilly said, "This is far enough. Go ahead, Sam."

The man disappeared up a winding path, and a moment later a door opened briefly, shooting forth a shaft of lamplight. "Let's go," Reilly said and prodded Meade with the gun.

The house was low and square, but no light showed and darkness hid it beyond Meade's identification. When they mounted a low porch, the door opened and Reilly gave Meade a push, sending him stumbling inside.

He squinted his eyes against the sudden brightness, and it was a few seconds before he identified the people in the room. Meade said, "Jules, you really get around, don't you?"

"Better sit down, Meade," Buckley murmured and toed a chair around.

Murray Sinclair lay on his bed, pale but wide awake. Marilee Hart occupied a chair along the wall, and Jim Hardesty squatted by the fire.

After Meade sat down, Jules Buckley said, "Sorry if Reilly and Sam gave you a scare, Meade, but we couldn't take a chance. You can see why, can't you?"

"Frankly—no," Meade said, and looked at Reilly. "The next time you pull a gun on me, you'd better use it."

"Don't be so touchy," Reilly said and went to the stove to pour himself some coffee. Murray Sinclair shifted on the bed, and Meade looked at him.

"Did I get you bad, Murray?"

The tall man seemed surprised, then said, "I'll come out of it, Meade. I still can't figure out how I missed you though."

"You were scared, Murray. And that made two of us."

For a moment no one spoke, then Murray raised

a hand and absently rubbed the blankets. "Yeah," he said. "I guess I was at that."

Buckley's voice was mild. "Better tell Meade why he's here, Murray."

"I suppose," Murray said, "although I'm not much for this kind of talkin'."

"I can make a close guess as to why you're all here," Meade said and gave each one a long glance. "You're plotting to throw Great Northern interests for a loop."

"That's right," Buckley admitted and smiled. "No one wanted to put anything over on you, Meade, but this has been hatching for a long time."

"Biting the hand that feeds you," Meade said flatly. "All right, I'm through with Great Northern and I think the powers that run it are basically dishonest, but I still have enough brains to realize that it's made the country prosperous."

"That," Jim Hardesty murmured, "is where we hope to convince you otherwise."

"I got tough when I shouldn't have," Murray said, "but, Meade, you had a strike against me and I couldn't convince you otherwise." Murray motioned to Sam, who tossed him a sack of makings. After rolling and lighting his smoke, Murray said, "For three years I've been holdin' out, but the time has come when a man has to use his brains instead of a rifle. That's where you come in, Meade. You're educated and smart, and you know the ins and outs of this financial set-up. You'd be able to spot a crack that the rest of us would miss."

"I don't think I want to spot it," Meade said flatly. "I don't own anything here, Murray. What have I to gain by bucking Dan Conover?"

"Haven't you ever done anything just for the principle of the thing?"

"Not very often, Murray. A long time ago I learned that business doesn't operate on principles. It operates on the ambition of a handful of men."

"Was it ambition that made you quit Great Northern, Meade?" Marilee Hart's voice was soft, and when Meade looked at her, she had a smile around her mouth and in her eyes.

He said, "That was one I caught myself up in, wasn't it?"

Some of the tension seemed to drain off then, and Jim Hardesty said, "Meade, come in with us."

He stood up then and felt for a cigar, but he had none. Jules Buckley offered one and a light, which Meade accepted. His heavy face was thoughtful, but at last he shook his head. "I can sympathize with what you want and are trying to do, but I can't go along with it. Dan Conover is going to be my father-in-law. You can see how it is, can't you?"

Buckley sighed deeply. "All right, Meade—all

right." He glanced at Sam Sinclair. "Give him his gun back."

Sam lifted it from his belt and tossed it. Meade caught it and spread the spring, then nestled it under his left arm. Reilly opened the door, and Meade stepped to the threshold. Jim Hardesty said, "I don't guess I have to tell you to keep your mouth shut, do I, Meade?" He looked steadily at the big man, then dropped his glance, murmuring, "I didn't think I would."

Meade stepped out, and the door closed behind him. He listened to the bar slide into place, then made his way cautiously down the darkened path to the back street.

Walking slowly to favor his leg, Meade listened to the sounds of Lode Street, one block to his right. Turning at the corner, he approached Lode, and once on it, moved slowly through the milling men until he came to the hotel.

A dozen men lounged in the lobby, their talk a low murmur as he passed through and slowly mounted the stairs to the upper hall. He inserted his key, then pushed the door open and went inside.

With the door closed, the room was dark; only minor light came in through the front window. As he fumbled for the lamp, his nose picked up a faint scent, and Allene Gruen said, "Don't light it, Meade."

He paused with the match in his hand, then

wiped it on the underside of the table and lifted the glass chimney. Lamplight's soft glow filled the room, and he turned to her, then paused.

She rose quickly, and her dressing gown rustled. "You like to have your own way, don't you?" She shrugged and moved between him and the lamp, and the light passed through the thin material, outlining clearly the long taper of her legs.

"What do you want, Allene?" Meade asked.

She stood that way for a moment, then said, "I got tired of waiting, Meade."

"Don't give me that," he said. "You've got Hardesty. How much more do you want?"

For an instant shocked surprise showed clearly on her face, then she masked it with a smile and came closer. "So you know. Do you hold a woman's indiscretions against her?"

"Get to the point," Meade said, slightly ill at ease and wondering if he was covering it cleverly.

Allene's smile deepened, and she took another step toward him, placing herself only inches away from him. "Can't you see the point, Meade?" She touched his arms, then her hands ran lightly to his shoulders and around his neck.

Her lips were moist and compelling, and when he put his hands on her hips, her flesh was feverish through the thin dressing gown. After a moment she pulled her head back slightly, barely parting their lips. "You're wasting kerosene," she murmured.

When he turned away from her he did so roughly, for her demands were strong and chiseled at his resistance. Her laugh rippled in the silence of the room, and she went back to the deep chair. She crossed her legs, and the whiteness of her thigh peeked through the fold in her gown. She said, "I must be getting old."

"You'd better go," Meade said and patted his pockets for a cigar, then remembered that he was out. Crossing to the small end table, he opened a fresh box and stuffed a half dozen in his shirt pocket.

She cocked her head to one side and regarded him intently. "Are you human, Meade?"

"Very," he said and peeled the wrapper from his cigar. He bent over the lamp chimney for his light.

"You make me wonder," Allene said and smiled in her wise way.

"Look," Meade said. "You've been after me in one way or another for a year, and it's been honest and just fast enough to be interesting, but this isn't. Now will you get out of my room?"

Her full lips pulled down into a slight pout, then she rose with graceful slowness and moved toward him again. She placed her hands against his chest. She caught her lower lip between her teeth and looked at him, the invitation clear in her eyes.

"I don't give up easy, Meade. Not when I want something." Raising herself slightly, she pressed her lips against his for a heartbeat, then laughed and stepped back.

"Good night," Meade said and went to the door, opening it for her.

She stood there in the center of the room with the lamplight behind her, then said, "Well, I tried." Taking two steps toward the door, she stopped and her smile faded. Meade wore a look of momentary puzzlement, then looked into the hall.

Cord Butram and Dan Conover stood there, and on Conover's face there was something decidedly unpleasant. Conover removed the thin cigar from between his lips and stepped into the room. "Wait in the hall, Cord," he said and fastened angry eyes on Meade Bigelow.

"It's not what you think," Meade said quickly.

"Isn't it?" Conover's voice was icy. "Meade, you have a guilty conscience. This shatters my faith in you completely."

"Now wait a minute—"

Conover held up his hand in the manner of a man trying his best to be reasonable. "Meade, I came here with the intention of apologizing and asking you to reconsider your earlier decision, but in view of the *tête-à-tête*

I have interrupted, I withdraw my intention."

"You're a great conclusion-jumper, aren't you?" Meade said tightly.

Conover's eyebrow ascended. "Am I?" He glanced at Allene Gruen. "Pull your gown together, woman, and stop exposing your limbs in that shameless manner!" He focused his black eyes on Meade Bigelow. "I have no wish to involve my daughter in a scandal, Meade, but this night of pleasure will not go unpunished. I'll see to it that Jim Hardesty is informed, and I'm sure that he will find suitable reward for this—this escapade."

"No!" Allene said suddenly.

"Be quiet!" Conover snapped, not glancing at her. "Bigelow, I would suggest that you waste no time in leaving the country."

"You're a sly one," Meade murmured. Allene moved toward Dan Conover and grabbed him by the coat, half spinning him around.

"You tricked me!" she snapped. "You said you only wanted to break up June's attachment to him. Dan, you lied to me right down the line."

"You are insane," Conover said coldly. "What story are you inventing now to soothe your shame? Release my coat."

"Wait a minute," Meade said and pushed Allene away from Conover. "Just what is this?"

"He came to me earlier," Allene said in a rapid run of words. "He wanted me to make love to you—like this, so he and Cord could walk in and then he would have a reason to break you and June up. Only he lied, Meade. He really wanted to turn Jim and you against each other. I think he wants Jim to kill you for this!"

"I've heard enough," Conover snapped and wheeled toward the door, but Meade took a long step and blocked him.

Conover tried to duck past Meade, but the big man collared him and spun him into the room. "You had better let me out, Meade." His voice was low and threatening.

"Not yet," Meade said softly and took a step toward the man. "You wanted Jim Hardesty killed, Dan. Why?"

"You're imagining things," Conover said, recovering some of his poise. "Clymer has always had it in for Jim. The whole town knows it."

"We'll let that pass," Bigelow said. "What about me, Dan? Why all this just for me? Is it important that I turn up dead?"

"I tell you she's lying," Conover snapped, giving Allene a scathing glance. "A woman like her will stoop to anything."

"Let's let that go for the time being," Meade suggested. He counted on his fingers. "First, there was Garvey saying that Murray killed Goofy, when Murray was not even there. Second, you got sore when I shot Murray, the logical thing for a man to do under the circumstances. Third, Jim Hardesty is a target for Clymer, who takes your orders right down the line. Now me. What are you afraid of, Dan? You been doing something you hadn't ought to be doing?"

"I won't listen to any more of this," Conover said and tried to step past Meade, but was blocked again. Conover's temper slipped then, and he swung a quick blow at Meade's head, but the big man jerked to one side, taking it across the neck.

"Cord!" Conover shrieked, and Meade hit the little man a blow that sent him cascading into the wall with enough force to dislodge a picture.

Meade hit him again on the rebound, and Conover cried out when blood began to drip into his beard. He swung his arms in short, chopping blows, and Meade felt the man's fist sting his face. He axed Conover in the stomach and put him down with an up-driving punch.

"Look out, Meade!" Allene shouted, and Meade whirled in time to go down beneath Cord Butram's charging weight. They rolled on the floor and came erect together, and on Butram's face there was something primitive and dangerous.

"I've always wanted to try you for size," Butram said and danced forward with the grace and footwork of a skilled boxer. He lanced out with his left, rocking Meade's head back, and then shifted balance and drove in with his right.

Meade blocked the blow and pivoted, seizing the arm near the shoulder. He bent quickly, and Butram sailed over Meade's head, splintering the bed rails when he landed.

Conover was on the floor by the wall, rolling and breathing noisily through his open mouth. Butram pushed himself erect and murmured, "I'll have to be careful, won't I, Meade?"

He circled Meade for a moment, then danced in, feinting for Meade's face, but delivering a stiff body punch instead. Meade dropped his open-handed guard and slipped his arm between Butram's body and his right elbow. Bringing his arm up quickly, Meade pivoted and grabbed Butram by the hair.

The sudden pain of the joint lock made Butram cry out, and Meade shoved him toward the open door and out into the hall. A crowd was beginning to gather on the upper landing, and they parted to let Bigelow through. At the head of the stairs, Bigelow released Butram and gave him a shove that sent him tumbling to the lobby floor below. Turning, Meade started for his room as Conover came out into the hall, bleeding and staggering from his beating. He saw Bigelow, gave one frightened bleat, and ran for the back stairs.

The crowd left the landing and began to crowd into the hall. Bigelow thought of Allene Gruen and moved ahead of them toward his room. He went in and closed the door, but still the voices came through the wall, murmuring curiously.

Allene stood against the wall, and Meade began to straighten the room. The bed was smashed, lying flat on the floor. At last he said, "Why, Allene?"

She shook her head and wouldn't look at him. "I'd better go," she said and moved past him, but he took her arm, halting her.

"Not now," he said. "There are still men in the hall."

"Does it matter?"

"You know it matters. Wait awhile." He released her and looked in the mirror over the marble-topped dresser. A slight discoloration was apparent on one cheek, and his left eye held a hint of puffiness.

"You want to know why he wanted Jim killed, don't you?" Meade turned around and looked at her when she spoke. Allene sat down in the chair. "Meade, I didn't know it was like that. I heard that Jim and Clymer had an argument. I didn't connect Conover with that at all."

"It happened too quick," Meade said. "Allene, Conover wanted Jim Hardesty dead, and I think you know why." She gave him a stricken look, and Meade added, "Now's the time to tell the truth. You take Dan's orders just like Clymer and the others. You wouldn't have tricked me tonight if that wasn't so."

She tried to hold Bigelow's eyes, but tears started in her own and she covered her face with her hands and sobbed. Meade waited until she fell silent. Allene said, "I love him, Meade, but I can't help myself. I just can't!"

"What does Jim know?" Meade prodded.

"Nothing," Allene said. "He and Murray are friendly, that's all. Jim—he's good with a gun, and Dan don't want him lined up with Murray against Great Northern."

"I don't understand it," Meade said, shaking his head. "That's not reason enough to have a man killed. Murray Sinclair is not a real threat to Great Northern. He's just a hard-headed miner who's bucking the tiger."

He paced up and down the room for a minute, then stopped. "What is Conover holding over your head, Allene? I want to know."

"Something that happened a long time ago," she murmured. "Before I married John Gruen. Conover knows about it, and he has threatened to tell Jim."

"All right," Meade murmured and took a cigar from his shirt pocket, then threw it away when he found it was crushed. He lit a fresh one from the box and puffed furiously until the ceiling was packed with gray smoke.

"I'll go now," Allene said softly. "I'm sorry, Meade, but I couldn't help myself."

"Better wait until the hall traffic dies down

a little," he said. "I'm not going to use the bed anyway."

She looked at him for a long moment, and her eyes were no longer bold and inviting. Settling on the broken bed, she lay back with an arm thrown over her eyes.

"You don't hate me, do you, Meade?"

"No," he said. "Why should I? People have to look out for themselves. You did what you thought was best for you."

"Thank you," she said, then sat up, propped on her elbow. "What will happen now, Meade?"

"We've both lost, I think." He tapped his cigar to remove the ashes and replaced it in the corner of his mouth. "Conover will be sure that Jim knows about this. I don't know what he'll say to you, Allene, but he'll be speaking to me with a gun."

She settled back on the bed and said nothing. He glanced at her, then retrieved his hat from the floor and turned the lamp down low. He set the spring lock to snap when he closed the door and went out and down the stairs.

The street was still thronged with milling, laughing men, but Meade did not notice them. He turned on the side street and the lane that led to Amy Falcon's cabin.

Chapter Nine

Before Meade entered the lane leading to Amy Falcon's cabin, he paused to check the time. A quarter after twelve. He walked slowly, limping, because his bruised and torn leg burned steadily.

There was no sign of a light, and he rapped on the door. A moment later he heard a shuffling inside, then Amy said, "Who is it?"

"Meade."

The bolt slid back, and he stepped inside, bumping her suddenly. "I'll light a lamp," she said and moved away from him, walking unerringly in the darkness. He waited until she scratched a match and touched it to the wick. When the chimney settled, the flame steadied and shadows leaped against the walls.

She wore a faded blue robe that fit her snugly, and her braids were wrapped around her head. Sleep made her eyelids heavy, and she turned to the stove to stoke the fire, filling the coffee-pot at the sink.

"I'm in trouble," Meade said. "Sorry I had to get you up."

"That's all right," she murmured. She had laid a gun on the table, and it caught his attention when she brushed it aside to set two cups down.

"I didn't know you had that," Meade murmured.

"Once a miner came with a bottle of whisky and some ambition," Amy said. "I bought it the next day." She sat down at the table and crossed her arms. The front of her robe was open at the throat, and the lamp threw deep shadows in the valley between her breasts. "What kind of trouble, Meade?"

"A woman," Meade said bluntly, not knowing exactly how to tell her. "Dan Conover and Cord Butram walked in on me."

"Oh," Amy murmured. She let the silence stretch out for a moment, then rose and pulled the coffee-pot to the back of the stove. She came back to the table and sat down again. Pushing the sleeves of her robe to the elbows, she sat and rubbed her forearms.

"Jim Hardesty will be after me with a gun. That was the idea, Amy—to make Jim think I—" He spread his hands and let the rest die unsaid.

"Allene Gruen?" She looked at him, and he met her eyes squarely.

"You know about her and Jim?"

"You can't keep a thing like that quiet," Amy said. "What are you going to do, Meade?"

"I don't know," he admitted and scrubbed his cheek with the flat of his hand. "Amy, you don't think that I—"

"Of course not, you fool," Amy said. "I know you, Meade. Much better than you think I do."

"I guess that's why I came here," Meade said

and lifted the coffee-pot from the stove when it gurgled loudly. He bent over her to fill her cup, then cradled his own between his big hands.

"Conover and I had a fight," he told her. "Cord Butram got in on it, and I threw him down the hotel steps." He shook his head slowly. "I don't want to fight Jim Hardesty, Amy."

"I know," Amy said and reached across the table to touch his hand. "Meade, what can you do now?"

Meade doubled his fist and hit the table. "Fight him! That's all there is left to do—Conover arranged that neatly enough." He unclenched his fist and rubbed the table top. "He'll be killing mad when the news gets to him. There won't be any talking—just shooting. Dammit, I like Jim!"

"He can't shoot you if he can't find you," Amy said. She looked at him, and Meade slowly raised his head. "I have extra blankets. I'll fix you a pallet on the floor."

"You're talking crazy," Meade told her. "For God's sake, Amy, if anyone found out your reputation wouldn't be worth a plugged nickel."

"I don't want to see you dead," Amy said flatly, and he noticed a firmness in her voice that had been absent before. "I won't argue with you, Meade." She went to a wall closet and took down three heavy blankets and spread them on the floor. "In the morning I'll talk to Murray and we'll try to convince Jim of what really happened. If he loves her, he'll believe her when she tells him Conover planned it to be this way."

"But will she tell him the truth?" Meade asked. "Conover has something on her, Amy."

Amy paused with a pillow between her teeth, shaking a clean case on it. She tossed this at the head of Meade's blankets and said, "She will if she loves him. If she doesn't then you're no worse off than you are right now with Conover and Hardesty against you."

"How did I get into this?" Meade asked. "What's going on that I don't know about, Amy?"

"You'll have to find that out for yourself," she said and cupped her hand around the lamp. The darkness was sudden and heavy, and Meade sat down to worry off his boots. He shed his coat and gun harness, then stripped off his shirt and settled for the night.

He heard the shucks rustle as Amy moved on her bed. Meade said, "Thanks, Amy."

For a moment he thought she was not going to reply, then she said, "I'm not doing it for thanks, Meade."

The silence turned thick in the room, and from Lode Street the sounds came softly, muted and very far away. A knot popped in the stove, and Amy stirred restlessly; then all was quiet.

Conover paused in the alley in the rear of the hotel, his face aching painfully from the drumming of Meade Bigelow's fists. A sickness

130

squeezed his stomach, but after a few minutes, that passed and the night air revived him.

His clothing was rumpled now, and he felt along the shoulder seam, discovering a long rent in the broadcloth. He had no hat; he had lost his in the scuffle.

Working his way along the dark and littered alley, Conover stumbled over a man's outstretched legs and fell heavily. He cursed in a thin voice, and the man stirred, sitting up.

To gain his feet, Conover put out a hand to brace himself and contacted the cold slickness of a whisky bottle tucked in the man's belt. The man reacted instantly, fastening a heavy hand on Conover's lapel, jerking him to his knees again.

"You son'vabitch—stealin' my bottle, huh?" A fist came out of the darkness and cracked Dan Conover across the bridge of the nose. He cried out in surprised rage and pain and hit back, catching the drunk in the chest.

The man fell back against some empty barrels, and Conover hastily got to his feet. He kicked out at the man, wringing a drunken grunt from him. Then a vicious mood seized Conover, and he began to kick in earnest. The man cried out when Conover's sharp, pointed shoes tattooed his kidneys, and when Conover tired of listening to it, he silenced the man with a blow at the base of the skull.

For a long time he stood there, staring at the

dark shadow on the ground, then turned and stumbled free of the alley's darkness. Once on the side street where he lived, he hurried home, and rang loudly, impatient when Hattie failed to answer promptly.

As soon as the door opened, he hurried in to his study, the colored woman following closely at his heels, saying, "Mr. Conover, what happened to your face? Mr. Conover!"

At his study door he wheeled so suddenly that Hattie came to a startled halt. "Ask my daughter to come here immediately," he snapped and slammed the door in the woman's face.

He poured brandy into a snifter and, dipping his handkerchief into it, bathed the cuts on his face, wincing as the sting hit him. A moment later he heard June's hurried steps, and the study door opened.

"Hattie told me—"

"Never mind that!" Conover said flatly. He turned to face her, and June gasped when she saw the darkly bruised cheek and the cut over his eye. "Your fiancé gave me this tonight," he said and watched the unbelief come into her face.

"Do you think I would lie to you?" He laughed bitterly. "I wish I could, just to spare you the humiliation and disgrace of ever having known such a man."

"What are you talking about?" she asked. "What happened?"

132

"You have no idea," Conover said. "I saw Meade walking down the street to the hotel, and wishing to patch up our differences, followed him. He entered his room, and when I opened the door, he had a guest—a woman."

"I don't believe it," June said flatly. "Meade isn't like that. What kind of woman, Father?"

"Please," he said. "I don't wish to discuss it with you."

"Father," she said, "I'm a grown woman about to be married. I don't think you're going to shock me."

"She—she had her limbs exposed," Conover said and poured himself a drink, shooting veiled glances at his daughter.

June stood motionless, the inner battle clear in her eyes. "I—Meade would have to confess this to me himself," she said.

"I forbid you to speak to him," Conover said. "Besides, there is a man who loves this woman. I imagine he will know best how to handle Meade Bigelow."

When her father turned his back to her, June sat down in one of the leather-covered chairs. She said, "You're a very proper man, Father, and I'm not sure what happened, but I believe in Meade."

He whirled and snapped, "I have forbidden you to speak to him. Now I have nothing further to say about the matter."

"But I have," June said softly. "I don't know

what it is, but you never wanted to see me kiss Meade or even think about me kissing him. I remember when I was fourteen and you caught me kissing the grocer's boy. Your belt left marks on me that I still carry."

He threw his whisky glass into the corner, where it shattered. "Dammit," he shouted. "There is proper conduct that we must observe if we are to remain cultured. I cannot be responsible for the loose moral habits of others, but I refuse to allow my daughter to lie in a sinner's bed."

"I'm going to ask Meade," June said. "I know you, Father, and your conception of what constitutes a sin is somewhat warped." She stood up and moved to the door while he watched her with shocked eyes. She paused there to add, "Good night. I hope your face does not hurt too badly."

She closed the door after her, and Conover stared at the panel. He took another drink and sat down behind the desk, his face severely composed. Finally he smiled and took another bowler from the closet. A moment later he left the house, cutting toward another back street.

After walking the length of it, he came to an alley and cut across to Lode, then began a methodical search for Jim Hardesty. He paused before the lighted windows, searching the crowd, then saw him leave the porch of Karen's Saloon.

Cutting across the traffic, Conover caught the

man in the middle of the block. "Hardesty! Wait there, Jim!"

Hardesty pulled up short and turned as Conover hurried up. A smile spread across the ex-marshal's face when he saw the bruises decorating Conover's cheekbone and eye. "Looks like you got yourself into something, don't it, Mr. Big?"

"Yes," Conover said smoothly. "I want to talk to you, Hardesty, about a very delicate matter."

"Go ahead and talk," Hardesty said and shook out his sack of tobacco.

"I—ah, quite by accident, I went to Meade Bigelow's room tonight on business. When I walked in, I found him and a woman together. She—ah, had—I mean, was scantily attired."

Hardesty stopped rolling his smoke and held his hands poised over the paper. "Spit it out, Conover!"

"It was Allene Gruen," Conover said and stepped back when he read the sudden flare in Jim Hardesty's eyes.

"All right, Mr. Big," Hardesty said very softly. "I'm going to find out, and if this is a lie, then you're going to be a dead man." He whirled and stepped into the dusty street.

"I'm telling you the truth!" Conover called after him and then smiled before he turned and walked rapidly toward Heavy Pearl's and the private entrance.

Hardesty crossed the lobby and took the stairs two at a time. At Meade Bigelow's door he tested the knob and found it locked, then he backed off three paces and hit it with his shoulder. The lock tore from the jamb and sailed across the room, and the door banged against the wall.

The lamp was still low, and Allene sat up suddenly on Meade's wrecked bed. Something bleak and dangerous crossed Jim Hardesty's face, and he hooked the door with his heel, slamming it behind him.

"Where is he? I want to kill him!"

"What for?" Allene asked in a tired voice. "Because of what Conover told you?"

"Isn't that enough?" Hardesty's voice cracked a little. "Jesus Christ, don't you have the decency to get out of his bed afterward?"

She got up then and walked across the room, her bare legs flashing through the gap in her dressing gown. "It's all a lie, Jim. That's the truth—believe it or not."

"What's the truth and what's a lie?"

"That I was here with Meade—that's the truth. That anything was wrong, that's the lie."

He snorted through his nose. "You think I believe that?"

Her shoulders rose and fell. "Believe what you want to believe then. I've told you all I can, Jim."

Her defeated voice cut through his anger, and he moved deeper into the room. She had her back to him, and he touched her gently on the shoulders, but she didn't turn around to face him.

"Allie," he said softly. "What happened? Why? Can't a man ask that?"

"The reasons go a long way back," she said. "Conover wants you to kill Meade, Jim. He knew that you would do it if you thought Meade and I—" She moved her shoulders away from his hands. "What's the use, Jim? I'm in too deep."

"I don't understand this, and I'm trying to," he said. "How can Dan Conover tell you what to do?" He took her by the arms and pulled her around to face him, forcing her chin up with his hand. "Allie, there comes a time when a man has to know the truth no matter how it hurts. If I didn't love you, do you think I would care?"

"And because I love you I can't tell you. *I can't!*"

"Do you want me to believe Conover and kill Meade? I got a right, you know."

She shook her head. "No, Jim. Meade fell into a trap and got caught. Nothing happened. Believe that because it's the truth."

"Then what are you doing here now?"

"There were men in the hall after Meade fought Dan and Cord Butram. He didn't want them to see me leave his room like this."

"All right," Jim said and blew out a gusty breath. "All right, Allie. But one way or another I'm going to find out what Dan has on you."

"Please," she said quickly. "Let it alone, Jim." She looked at him for a moment, then threw her arms around him and pressed herself against him. "You've been the only real thing in my life, and I can't stand the thought of losing you. Please, forget about it and we'll talk about tomorrow."

He disengaged her arms and moved away from her. "It's no good, Allie. We start honest with each other, or we can end it here and now. I want to know."

"All right!" she snapped. "Dan Conover knew me ten years ago in Kansas City, before I married John Gruen." She looked at him, and her courage broke. She turned away from him to add, "I worked in Heavy Pearl's house on River Street." She stopped talking, and silence filled the room until it was almost stifling. When she whirled to face him, her eyes were wise and a crooked smile lifted one corner of her full lips. "I was high class—the five-dollar trade."

Tears began to well up along her lower lids. "You wanted to know, dammit! Now you know so get out of here and leave me alone!"

"Allie—"

"Go on! Get out of here!"

"No, Allie," Hardesty said and fashioned a cigaret to get control of his thoughts. She turned her head and watched him, and he added, "It hits a man hard, but it's just 'cause it was so sudden. I wondered why you married John—him bein' so much older than you. Now I reckon I know."

"He was kind and decent to me," Allie said. "He never reminded me of what I was, and because of him I forgot about it—until Dan Conover came here and recognized me." She studied his face in the sudden flare of the match, and their eyes met over the flame.

"I guess you hate me now," she murmured.

"No," he said. "I don't hate you. This don't change anything, Allie. I guess I can understand how a girl could get into that kind of a business. Things can go tough for anybody."

"Things weren't tough," she said, and this brought his attention up sharply.

"What did you say?"

"I said they weren't tough." She pressed her fists against her temples and pushed until the skin was tight and shiny against her cheekbones. "There's something wrong with me, Jim. I know there is. It's like a disease, the craving."

She closed her eyes, and her knees bent, slowly at first, then more rapidly as she neared the floor. She rocked back and forth with her eyes closed, tears squeezed from between the tight-shut lids. "Help me, Jim," she pleaded in a soft and lost voice. "Please help me."

Meade Bigelow woke to the sound of water splashing in a small room built onto the back of the cabin. For a moment, he couldn't place this

139

sound. He was sitting upright in his blankets when Amy Falcon came out, her blue robe clinging wetly to her.

"A quarter to six," she said and smiled. "I'll fix your breakfast."

He put on his shirt and folded the blankets while she fixed the meal, then went into the back room to wash his face. The sun, just over the horizon, threw a sharp light onto the land, and there was no sound other than the chatter of two tree squirrels on a high limb.

Using her comb and brush, he slicked his hair down wetly, and when he came into the main room, she had wriggled into her dress. Frying bacon laid a heady aroma over the room, and the coffee-pot bubbled on the back of the stove.

"I could cut wood for the meal," he murmured and drew a quick smile.

She patted his arm and pointed to a chair. "Just keep out from underfoot." He sat down, and she cracked eggs into the skillet. Shooting him a glance over her shoulder, she said, "I think that in the light of day you consider your staying here all night a little bit foolish."

This brought his head up smartly, and his eyes widened in surprise. "What do you have? A crystal ball?"

She laughed and flipped the eggs. "I know you, Meade. You're a foolish man when it comes to a woman's honor." She smiled and added, "The female has learned to snare the male with this chivalrous feeling, by placing her honor in his hands, then demurely suggesting that he save it."

"You're not like that, is that it?"

He spread his hands apart so she could set the plate down. She took a chair across from him and gave him a mischievous glance. "Meade, if I was going to holler, I'd wait until afterward to have something to holler about."

"That," he said, "is shameless."

"Yes," she admitted, "but more practical, besides being fun."

"I give up," he said and ate his breakfast. They dawdled for an hour over the coffee, and then Amy rose to carry the dishes to the sink.

A restlessness began to push Meade, and he moved around the cabin, unable to sit or stand still. Amy dried her hands and looked out the window, then stiffened.

"Meade," she said, and when she looked at him her face was pained. "I'm sorry, Meade."

He gave her a puzzled look, then started to walk toward the window, but stopped when someone knocked on Amy's door. She opened it, and June Conover stood on the threshold.

She saw Meade, and her eyes grew round. Then she whirled and began to run up the path. "You're a fool!" Amy called after her, but the girl only quickened her pace.

Closing the door, Amy leaned her shoulders against it and kept her head down.

"How did she know?" Meade said softly, then glanced at Amy Falcon.

Her shoulders began to shake, and she turned away from him, her forehead against the door. He knew she was crying. "Everything I touch," she said, "turns out this way. Everything."

Meade touched her gently, and she came around as quick as a released spring, lacing her arms around him. He touched her hair and murmured, "It's all right, Amy. We'll work it out."

His voice was soft and even and convincing, but in his eyes there was a deep-rooted worry.

Chapter Ten

At eight o'clock Meade Bigelow left Amy Falcon's cabin and walked rapidly toward Lode Street. The day promised to be warm, but he wore his coat to cover up the gun riding beneath his left armpit.

Lode was nearly vacant when Bigelow came to the end and stopped. The saloon seemed deserted, and there were only two stores open, the saddlemaker's and the feed store at the end of the block. Meade moved on, his boots echoing hollowly along the boardwalk. When he came to the hotel, he stopped again.

Jim Hardesty sat on the porch, his feet on the railing. He took the cigaret from his mouth and spun it into the street, then put his feet down and stood up. For a moment, both men looked at each other. Then Meade said, "How is it going to be, Jim?"

"Suit yourself about it," Hardesty said evenly. "I'm not particular."

"You start it," Meade said flatly.

Hardesty's lips changed, and he seemed to ponder this thing. "Do I have a reason, Meade?"

"No," Bigelow said softly. "You don't, but I don't imagine I can convince you otherwise."

"I'd hate to kill you," Hardesty murmured.

"You could have laid for me in an alley, Meade. I've got you beat, and you know it."

"That's not for me," Meade said. "Come on, Jim. Let's get it over with."

Hardesty stared long and gravely at Bigelow, then moved his head slightly and looked past the big man. Dan Conover and Cord Butram came to the end of Lode Street from Conover's house, and when they saw the two men, they halted abruptly and waited.

Hardesty said, "The vultures are waiting to gobble up the spoils, Meade." He pushed his chair aside and stepped down to the walk level where Bigelow waited. Hardesty raised his hands shoulder-high. "The intentions are peaceful, Meade. Allene told me a story, and I believe it."

The breath left Meade in a windy sigh, and he raised a hand to his face, surprised to find that he was sweating. He grinned, and Hardesty murmured, "I'll treat you to the drinks, Meade."

"I can use one," Bigelow admitted and walked across the street with the tall man.

On Karen's porch they paused to survey the street. Conover and Cord Butram were hurrying along the walk now, but they did not glance over to where the two men stood.

"I'll bet he's chewin' his cud and wonderin' what the hell happened that we didn't pull on each other." Hardesty's voice was quietly thoughtful. He turned and brushed the doors

144

aside, and Meade followed him. Hardesty bellied against the bar and slapped the polished surface until Lonigan came from the back room, his eyes red from lack of sleep.

"Can't you sonsabitches give a man a little peace?" he asked, and slid two glasses on the bar. He poured and then leaned on his crossed arms, eager for talk.

"Peace is for old men and fools," Hardesty murmured and studied the sunlight streaming through his whisky. "Give me the tiger to buck."

"That makes for a sore head," Lonigan muttered. "Conover's too big for you, Jim. The same goes for you, Bigelow."

"Nothing is too big," Meade said. He reached out and hooked a bowl of peanuts. There was a handful left in the bottom of the two-quart dish. "Was this full last night?"

"Damn gluttons," Lonigan said. "Buy a nickel beer and eat a dollar's worth of free lunch."

"Great Northern is like that full bowl of peanuts," Meade said. "Be a tough job for one man to sit down and gobble it all, but turn five men loose on it and it won't last long."

Hardesty tossed off his drink and leaned on his elbow, facing Meade. "Now that's mighty interestin', Meade. You change your mind?"

"Maybe," Meade said softly. "You think Murray would talk to me?"

"Let's find out," Hardesty said and tossed a

fifty-cent piece on the bar before going out. They walked a block before turning off Lode onto a narrow side street.

The Great Northern mine on the hill rumbled and growled as men ripped silver from the mountain's breast. They crossed another street running parallel with Lode, then cut across a vacant lot to a small lane.

Houses and cabins sat at a distance from each other in this tree-dotted grove. Hardesty led the way up a narrow path and rapped on a door.

Sam Sinclair opened it, looking surprised when he saw Meade Bigelow. He stepped aside, and they filed in; Sam kicked the door shut behind them.

Murray was propped up in bed, and Jean, one of Heavy Pearl's girls, was feeding him soup. Murray said, "Pull up a chair, Meade." He pushed the bowl away, and the girl carried it to the sink, giving Meade a long glance in passing.

After rolling a cigaret, Hardesty said, "Conover tried to put salt on Meade's tail last night, Murray. He didn't like it." He told Murray about the fight Meade had had with Conover and Cord Butram, skipping completely the happenings in Meade's hotel room.

When he finished, Meade said, "I've changed my mind, Murray. I think we can break Great Northern together."

"Well now," Murray said, obviously relieved.

He stirred and fingered a pleat in the blanket. "I don't know where to start, Meade, but if you're looking for that silver that Great Northern is missing—I've got it."

"You what?"

"Conover is robbing his own wagons," Murray said. "I know that sounds crazy, but when I started getting the blame for it, I decided to find out who the hell *was* doing it. Clymer, Garroway, and Garvey, masquerading as the Sinclairs, have been doing the robbing."

"And one of them killed Goofy Harris," Meade said. "You know which one, Murray?"

He shrugged. "I always thought Clymer did it. He was the wild one, and the others took orders from him. Conover was Clymer's boss— you know that—so whatever robbin' there was, Conover was in on it."

Hardesty puffed on his cigaret, then ground it out in a saucer. "I've figured out why Conover wanted Clymer to gun me. Allene and I—well, we have an understandin', but like a fool, I told her about Murray knowin' where the silver was. She told Conover, and he sicked Clymer onto me."

"Don't tell her anything more then," Murray said flatly.

"Now wait a minute," Hardesty said, but Murray's eyes told the ex-marshal that argument would get him nowhere. "All right, Murray. Have it your own way."

147

"It figures," Murray said, "that Dan wanted you dead or gone because he was afraid Hardesty might say something to you, Meade."

"I'm not that important," Bigelow said. "There must be something else."

"There's nothing else," Murray contradicted. "Meade, you built Great Northern into an empire, and you know all about how it was put together. You've got the education and you're smart, and if you wanted to, you could take Great Northern apart, piece by piece."

Bigelow glanced at Hardesty, and the ex-marshal nodded. "He's right, Meade. You're the kingpin."

"I've been running things up until now," Murray said, "but I'll step down for you, Meade. Just say the word."

From outside a horse approached the cabin, and Sam moved to the front window. "It's Reilly," he said and opened the door. Reilly dismounted and came in, stopping when he saw Meade Bigelow. He took the cup of coffee Jean handed him and leaned against the wall, a spare man with little to say at any time.

"What about it?" Murray prodded. "We need you, Meade, and you ought to be convinced now that Great Northern is a hog that takes what it wants and pushes anyone who gets in their road."

"I'm with you," Meade said and saw Murray's answering smile of relief. Reilly glanced at

Meade and grunted, but made no comment.

"We've hid the silver bars at Hart's logging camp," Murray said. "Marilee and Jules are with us all the way. They want out of this thing any way they can get out."

Meade shook his head. "We'll have to be careful, Murray, or we'll all end up without a shirt. We're not going to break this in a day. Neither will we do it by causing trouble with Great Northern."

"What do you figure?" Hardesty said. "Let me have a cup of that, Jean."

"The way the cartels are put together is the way they will have to come apart," Meade said. "Buying out is impossible because it would cost too much. They formed cartels by agreement. We have to get those same people to agree to break. It is only when they acknowledge the existence of a cartel that it exists in fact."

"That's a little fast or too deep or somethin'," Murray said.

"Look at it this way then," Meade suggested. "Barnum is none too happy the way things are, but he's not going to stick his neck out and go against the cartel. If we can get to Barnum and the others and make them see that they *can* still operate without Great Northern, I think we can break the country right open and raise the nickel beer to thirty cents."

"It all sounds like a lot of theory to me,"

Murray said dubiously. "What happens when Great Northern refuses to market Barnum's beef, or buy from him, and starts to drive in their own?"

"We play the game just like Great Northern played it," Meade said. "We'll block their attempts to relieve shortages and force them to accept our terms, which is free trade without a cut of the profits."

"All right," Murray said and looked at the others. "All of you agree that Meade is the boss from now on?"

They murmured and nodded, and then Reilly asked, "Tell me something, Meade—who owns all this?" He waved his hand at the surrounding country.

"I really don't know," Meade said solemnly. "Somebody does, that's for sure. The profits are going into someone's pocket, but I don't know who that is."

"Conover?" Sam suggested.

Meade shook his head. "No, and I'll tell you why. He didn't have the money to begin with so he had nothing to buy in with, except the first twenty thousand that formed the Silver City Land and Trust Company."

"Maybe," Hardesty murmured, "if we start shaking some of the apples off of this tree we may find out."

"The task would be simple then," Meade said.

"We could hit the whole deal where it would hurt most—at the top. Once you cut that off at the pocket, the rest falls apart pretty easy." He leaned back in his chair and fired up a cigar. "The government has passed laws governing corporations. You see, most of our company laws are based on English law. At one time it was possible to have a corporation where none of the members were liable for the corporation's debts. The early trading companies were formed under such rules and consisted of a large body of fluctuating individuals. A person who dealt with them didn't know who he was making a contract with or who he should sue if he wanted to claim default.

"I believe Great Northern comes under the jurisdiction of a Company Act governing corporations. It provides that no more than twenty men shall carry on a business for gain without registering. I believe that it's ten in the case of banking.

"You see, too much railroad building, the lingering cost of the war, overtrading, and inflated credit caused the panic of 1873. That began the hurried turning over of partnerships and the forming of corporations."

Meade looked from one to the other. "You understand?"

"Not a damn word of it," Sam said.

"I didn't either," Reilly admitted. Hardesty

shook his head when Meade glanced at him.

Murray said, "It don't make a damn whether we understand or not. As long as Meade knows what he's doing and can tell us, then we'll follow the orders."

Meade rose from the table and crossed to the woodbox to butt out his cigar. After putting on his hat, he moved to the door and said, "The best thing to do is sit tight for a few days and see what Conover is up to. He'll have to make a report to the governing board back East before he can take any drastic steps."

"It was my understanding that Conover headed the Great Northern board," Hardesty said. "You, Buckley, Barnum, Allendale, Olds, and Cartwright are on it."

"That's true," Meade told him, "but Great Northern is under the control of Silver City Land and Trust, which Conover also heads. Eastern money is behind that." He opened the door and stepped through, but before closing it, a thought struck him and he paused. "Murray, I think the reason Conover and I argued over the handling of you was because he couldn't afford to have you dead. I believe he knows that you have the silver and you're the only way he can get it back."

"I wondered when you'd figure that out," Murray murmured, and Meade grinned before closing the door behind him. He walked back to Lode Street and entered Karen's Saloon. There he idled his time away at the bar until it was noon and he saw Dan Conover go home for his dinner.

Crossing the street then, Meade went into the Silver City Trust Company office and found June in the back room, working over the books. She heard him enter, and when she saw him, stood up so quickly that she upset the papers, littering her desk.

"Get out of here," she said. "I've heard enough and seen enough. We have nothing to say to each other, Meade."

"It seems that there's a good deal to be said," he murmured and perched on the edge of her desk. She stepped back, recoiling from him.

"I didn't believe Father last night when he told me about you and that Gruen woman." She shook her head. "It was just too fantastic. But this morning—Meade, I don't want to talk about it."

Meade braced his hands on the edge of the desk. "June, this is our first big misunderstanding, and what we do about this one will be the key to our thinking and attitude throughout our lives. A man wants to listen to both sides before he makes up his mind."

He touched her pride, the sense of fairness she was so proud of. There was no friendliness in her face, and her eyes were reserved, but her chin came up and she said, "Very well, Meade. I'm ready to listen."

"Hardesty was after me last night, June. Your

father got me into that, but there's no point discussing it now. Anyway, Amy fixed blankets on the floor, and I stayed until someone could talk to Hardesty. As it worked out, no one had to, except Allene. That's all there was to it, June. Nothing like you think."

"You convict yourself with your own words," June said. "This morning I left the house early, to go to you and talk about what father told me. You weren't in your room, Meade. I couldn't find you anywhere. Then I began to think. When you're troubled, you don't come to me—you go to Amy Falcon. Don't deny it! I've watched you.

"It cost me to go to her, Meade, but I did, and when she opened the door, you were standing there." She clenched her fists and held them against her thighs. "That blonde slut had the gall to call after me! She's always wanted to get you in bed with her. Well, now she can keep you!"

"That's not so, June."

She tipped her head back and laughed. "Isn't it? Do you take me for a fool, Meade? I'm human, too, and had I been in her place—" June made a vague motion with her hands. "I know what I would have done. Now get out and don't come back, Meade."

He blew out a gusty breath and stood up, his hat in his hands. "All right, June. Have your own way about it. Someday you're going to find out, and I wonder what you'll say." He moved to the door and paused. "I'm wondering if I'll listen."

Meade walked rapidly through the outer office and stopped on the edge of the boardwalk. Through the glass window in Amy Falcon's restaurant, Meade saw her move back and forth along the counter and crossed the dusty street.

He went past the counter and into the back room. Ralphie was working the fry trade, and he grinned at Meade and went out. A moment later Amy came back, her face grave.

"It was no use talking, was it?"

"No," Meade said. "Things sometimes go that way, Amy."

Amy nodded and sat down at the table. She scrubbed a hand over her forehead and said, "She thinks I'm a whore, doesn't she? It isn't that she hates the thought of you spending the night in my cabin, Meade. She hates herself because that's what she has wanted to do and never dared."

"It's not that," Meade said quickly.

"It *is* that," Amy insisted. She gave him a brief glance and added, "I never wanted to hurt you, Meade, or get you tangled up like this. I just wanted to—" She waved her hand absently. "What the hell difference does it matter what I wanted now?"

Meade poured himself a cup of coffee, and Ralphie came back to fill three orders. When he went to the front, Meade said, "I talked to

Murray again, Amy. We're going to find out what Conover is up to. Whatever it is, it's not right." He sat down across from her and laced his hands around the cup. "For a long time I've thought that the dividends to Allendale and the others were not high enough, but according to the books, everything is on the square. Many a night I've pored over them at Great Northern, trying to find where the money is going, but I never could spot the leak."

"Then there is a leak?"

"I've suspected so," Meade murmured. "You told me once that someone must make the money, because none of it is spent in Silver City. Nickel beers, twenty-five-cent meals and haircuts—it all adds up, Amy, and a lot of it is my fault. As the ex-general super of Great Northern, I put the squeeze on for reduced prices and lower margin of profit." He grinned at her. "We damned near got into a beef over it once, remember?" He reached across the table and took her hands in his. "We should never quarrel, Amy. I think June was right. When I'm troubled, I come to you first. Why is that, Amy?"

"I—" She pulled her hands free of his and stood up, presenting her back to him. "I wouldn't know, Meade."

He did not understand this and stood up to go to her, but Ralphie came into the room and began bustling about the stove. Meade glanced at

Amy, then said, "I'll see you later," and went out.

He walked to the end of the street to the stable and saddled his horse. Boone Wylie came in and leaned against a stanchion, watching Meade. The stableman was a little man with the pouched-out cheeks of a chipmunk. His eyes were large and staring, and a three-day growth of whiskers bristled on his cheeks.

"Kind of come down off that high perch you was on, didn't you?"

"Some," Meade murmured.

"Seen 'em fall before," Boone said. "Always said you'd get too big someday and talk snappy to the big boss."

Meade mounted and moved toward the archway. Boone followed him at his stirrup. "Where'll I say you went, should anybody ask me?"

"Great Northern," Meade said. "I'm going to clean out my desk. Does that satisfy your curiosity?"

He didn't wait for an answer, just gigged the horse with his heels and took the climbing road toward the mine perched on the mountainside. The smelter was going full-blast, and a string of ore carts left the open maw of a tunnel, rolled around a curving track, and disappeared behind the smelter buildings.

Keeping the horse to a slow walk, Meade turned his thoughts toward June Conover and a way to change her mind. The hour-and-a-half ride passed quickly for him, and it was growing dark by the time he reached his office building. Lamplight made the windows pale.

At the building that housed his office, Meade dismounted, tied the horse, and went inside. He passed through a long room where a half dozen engineers labored, but no one spoke to him and he went on.

Cord Butram looked up from his work when Meade passed through his office. Butram said, "What the hell do you want, Meade?" His face was sullen, and he moved stiffly, still bruised from his flight down the hotel stairs.

"I'm cleaning out," Meade said and moved past him.

"Wait a minute!" Butram snapped and shoved himself erect. "You're through here."

"I'm through," Meade agreed. "And I won't be long."

"See that you aren't," Butram murmured and raised a hand to stroke his chin. There was a speculative look in his eye when he said, "You pulled a couple of pretty cute tricks on me last night. Something I hadn't seen before."

"I wrestled in college," Meade said. "Just leave me alone, Cord. I didn't come here for trouble."

"Sure," Butram said and stared at the door as Meade entered the office.

There was little in his desk that Meade wanted, a few books, which he stuffed into a saddlebag that he took from the closet. His bedroll was there, and his Winchester .45-75. He laid these on his desk and looked around the room, seeing nothing else that was his own personal property.

He gathered the gear under his arm and turned as the door opened. Cord Butram stepped in, and behind him, Garvey and Garroway entered with drawn guns. Garvey toed the door closed and leaned against it, a thin smile on his face.

"Meade," Butram murmured. "Let's see how good your tricks are when someone holds your arms." He nodded toward the two men with him, and they holstered their guns.

Garroway moved in first, and Meade hit him an axing blow that drove him back against Butram, but Garvey was quick and he grabbed Meade around the neck, bending him over with his weight.

Slanting a blow for his neck, Butram missed and hit Meade behind the ear, and he went to his knees. Garroway was on his feet and seized Meade's right arm, pulling him to his feet between them.

Butram said softly, "How tough are you, Meade?" and skewered him in the stomach with a punch that left the big man weak and gagging.

Chapter Eleven

Cord Butram's first blow made Bigelow gasp, although he had tensed his stomach muscles to take the punch. Garvey and Garroway held him erect, for his legs lacked the strength to support his weight, and Butram hit him again, this time under the heart.

Meade's mouth flew open in a soundless cry, and a deep pain shot through him. Laughing, Butram said, "No wrestling tricks, Meade. Just a little fun between you and me."

He cocked his fist again, and Meade threw his weight against the two men clinging to his arms. This took them by surprise, and he jackknifed at the waist and knees, then uncoiled, his boots catching Butram squarely in the chest.

The force drove Butram backward into the closed door with enough force to drive him through the thin mahogany center. He fell amid the splinters and rolled over, but did not get up immediately.

Without thinking, Garroway relaxed his grip, and Meade jerked free, shoving against Garvey to upset the man. They both fell heavily, and Meade rolled away as Garroway tried to kick him in the head.

In the other room, Butram was wheezing

badly and trying to claw his way erect, using the shattered door for support. Garvey was a wild man, trying to grab Meade, but Meade reached the rifle lying on his desk and wiped the lamp to the floor with the barrel.

The glass shattered suddenly, and for an instant there was half darkness. Then the burning wick caught in the puddle of coal oil, and a new flame began to grow. Garvey came around the desk after Meade, and the rifle barrel thumped against the side of his head and he fell heavily.

In the other room, Butram was yelling, and Garroway reached for his gun as Meade swung the muzzle toward him, working the lever rapidly. Garroway's gun was free of the holster and coming up when Meade shot. The heavy bullet caught the man high in the chest, lifting him off his feet.

Garroway fell, rolled over on his back, twitched once, then lay still. Meade turned the gun on Butram, but the man had whirled and was running through the other office, calling in a driving voice. Picking up his bedroll and gear, Meade turned to the window. With one circular motion of the gun barrel he wiped the pane from the frame. It was eight feet to the ground, and he tossed his gear through, heard it hit, then lowered himself and dropped.

His horse was where he had left it, and he ran toward it. There was no time to lash the bedroll in place, so he mounted and held it across his lap with the rifle. He kicked the horse with his heels and thundered down the winding road. Behind him, Butram's shout went up, but the sound soon faded.

A mile from town, Meade pulled off the road and screened by a thicket, fastened his roll and saddlebags, then mounted again. His stomach ached and breathing was still an uncomfortable chore, but he forgot that when he thought about Garroway on the floor with blood staining an ever larger patch on his chest.

He considered going to town, then decided against it, because Cord Butram would catch up a horse and make his report to Conover. Meade didn't want to meet the man and have to shoot him. Meade considered the position of marshal that was now open and decided that even if Garvey got the job, there would be nothing to fear, for under the charter, the marshal's authority went only as far as the edge of town.

Leaving the thicket, Meade turned north to cross the mountains and enter the cattle land. Through the rest of the fading daylight he kept to the narrow trails that hung like ladder rungs against the massive walls, and sundown found him over the ridge and beginning a descent on the other side.

With the light fading, the valleys below turned to a dark green, then black as a grayness enveloped the land. At a lonely distance, buildings huddled at the far end of a tear-shaped bench, and Meade made his way toward them.

The land here was gentler than on the other side, and pine grew thickly and the wild odor of the land was strong in his nostrils. Within a half hour there was darkness around him, but the trail was not too steep and he let the horse pick his own pace. The buildings in the distance sported lamps now, and the squares of the windows were like small blocks of gold against a velvet drape.

By seven, he was on the flats. He increased his pace, arriving at Barnum's ranch an hour later. The front door opened as Meade rode into the yard and dismounted; Meade tied the horse and walked to the porch.

The back end of a buggy was visible around the corner of the house, and Lige Barnum peered through the darkness at the bedroll lashed to Meade's horse. Glancing at the rifle Meade carried, he said, "Travelin' a little heavy, ain't you?"

"I may have a long way to go," Meade murmured.

"Come on in," Barnum urged. "Damn air's got a chill to it lately." He turned and went in. Meade followed him, setting his rifle in the hall corner.

Barnum went into the parlor, and Meade halted as Fred Allendale rose from an overstuffed chair and held out his hand. Meade's first surprise vanished, and he said, "A long drive for you, Fred."

"It's always worth it," Allendale said and sat down. Barnum crossed to the mantel and offered Meade a cigar from a glass humidor. After Meade got it going, he turned and leaned against the stone masonry.

This was a big room for a log house, and the varnished floor was covered with throw rugs. Barnum said, "Fred was bringing me up to date, Meade. Are you really through?"

"Finished," Meade admitted and told them about killing Garroway at the mine. Barnum and Allendale exchanged glances, but made no comment until Meade finished.

Allendale pulled his lower lip between thumb and forefinger. "Meade, I think you did just what Conover wanted you to do—step outside the law." He shook his head. "You'd better not go back to Silver City, Meade. If I was in Dan Conover's place now, I'd go for a United States marshal. He could swear out a warrant for Murray Sinclair's arrest for holding up the silver shipment and shooting Goofy Harris. Jim Hardesty is a fool to stick around; a charge against him could be trumped up easily. Now he's got you, Meade. You'll stay healthier if you spend some time in the hills."

Bigelow lighted a cigar and puffed for a

moment. "Fred, Murray didn't rob the shipment. Neither did he kill Goofy."

"So I heard," Allendale murmured. "Marilee Hart and Buckley seem positive of it. They stopped off on their way home this afternoon."

"Also," Meade said, "there were twenty men in Karen's when Clymer tried to knock Hardesty over. That was self-defense, and anyone would have a hard time proving otherwise."

"I disagree," Allendale said. "Meade, if I had an investment the size of Conover's to protect, I could get real cagey when it came to putting people out of the way. As chairman of three boards, Conover wields a great power; it might even extend to the courtroom and a judicial decision."

"Yeah," Meade said and smoked in silence for several minutes. When he moved, he did so slowly, favoring his right leg. Barnum frowned and asked, "Giving you trouble, Meade?"

"Aches," Meade said and dismissed it, but Barnum ignored Meade's attitude.

"Better let cookie have a look at it," Barnum said. "He's hell for curin' snakebite and gunshot wounds."

"All right," Meade said. "Later, maybe."

"Later, hell," Barnum said. "Put it off and it won't get done."

Meade laid his cigar on the edge of the mantel and limped from the room. Going down the hall, he entered the kitchen, and a wizened man turned to give him a sour stare.

"What have you got that's good for a bullet crease?" Meade asked.

"Whisky," the cook said quickly. "Taken internally, of course."

"How about taking a look at this?" Meade asked and unbuckled his belt. He turned so that the light fell on his thigh, and the old man peeled back the bandages.

"Say," he said. "That looks a mite red. Hurt much?"

"Aches all the time," Meade admitted. "Can you do anything with it?"

"Hate to diddle around," the cook said. "Damn thing might heal right up. Then again, you may get gangrene and have to take the leg off."

Meade grunted with disgust and pulled up his pants. Fastening his belt, he said, "I'll come back if it has to come off," and limped back to the parlor. Allendale and Barnum broke off their muted conversation, and Meade lowered himself into a chair.

Giving Lige Barnum a studious stare, Meade asked, "Are you still straddling the fence?"

"It's a good perch for tomcats," Barnum opined, "and so far it's been fine for me. Something nibblin' at you, Meade?"

"I've been thinking about the good old days of the three-dollar steak and everyone going broke or striking it rich." He switched his eyes from Barnum to Allendale and back again. "You ever think about it, Lige?"

The old man grew canny and began to talk around his point. "I give it some thought now and then. A man being his own boss is fine in some ways, but it has its disadvantages. Used to be that everyone was trying to hog the other fellow out, pushing here at this water, fighting over that piece of bench land." He chuckled. "It kept a man on his toes. Living like this makes a man shiftless and fat, like a hand-fed deer."

"That's not much of an answer," Meade murmured and rose to get his cigar from the mantel. After he touched a match to it, he sat down again and crossed his legs. "You spoke out pretty blunt at the last board meeting, Fred. Does a man have to ask you where your sympathy is?"

"No," Allendale said. "Frankly, Meade, I've believed in Murray when no one else would. Marilee and Jules Buckley feel the same way."

"Add a couple more to that—Jim Hardesty and Amy Falcon." Meade flicked ashes into a stand by his elbow. "We have quite a conspiracy going against Great Northern money."

"That can turn into something dangerous," Barnum warned. "Be careful, Meade. You're tackling a big tree with nothing stronger than a pocketknife."

"Sure," Meade murmured and studied his cigar.

"I'll tell you something, Lige. A few days ago I was making big money and I didn't give a damn how much the little man got pinched. Now I'm wearing another pair of shoes, and they pinch. Trouble hunted me and stamped down with both feet. I'm in this, Lige—up to my neck."

Barnum grew thoughtful. "I suppose a man like Dan Conover is like a cattleman who hogs and pushes until he's crowded everyone else out. Finally he gets to the point where he has control of something so big that he's afraid the least little wind will topple it. There's no doubt in my mind, or in Allendale's either, that Conover caused a run on the bank to get control of it. Everything was legal, you understand, but beneath that, there was some rottenness."

"Big business is never the cleanest kind of fight," Meade murmured and rose to throw his cigar into the fireplace. "You no doubt remember September of 1869, Black Friday, when the Gould-Fisk crowd attempted to corner the gold supply. After the price was forced up from 150 in the morning to 161½ at noon it took a nosedive to 133. In the scramble people and huge concerns went under. Finally the government broke the corner on the market by selling four million in gold. Jay Cooke and Company failed on September 18, 1873, and on the following day, several others collapsed, along with three huge New York banks. The resulting panic caused the Stock Exchange to close for thirteen days."

"We don't want that to happen here," Allendale said firmly. "Neither do I want another scandal like the Crédit Mobilier and the Union Pacific affair. I believe the only way clear of this thing without throwing the country into a panic is to force Conover in some way to sell out. His silent backers must be forced out also."

"That," Meade said, "is a whale of a chore. We'd have to tackle this thing from the top, and none of us know who the top is."

"I fully realize that," Allendale said. "If Great Northern begins to tremble, there will be a wild scramble of people trying to get out from under it, but the worse thing will be afterward, with all this lying there and the ownership obscured. These people won't wait, Meade. They'll begin to crowd and hog for themselves, and there'll be killings over it."

"It's my opinion," Meade said, "that the safest way to shave the trimming off this tree is to break up some of these cartel agreements that hold the combine together." He glanced at Lige Barnum. "I want to tackle the cattlemen first, Lige, because of the lot, they are the most independent and get along without Great Northern interests entirely."

Barnum shrugged. "Suppose we do break away, then what? What do we use for a market?"

"Denver," Meade said and held up his hand

as Barnum opened his mouth to protest. "All right, I'll concede that it's a long drive and over hellishly rough country, but it can be done. The margin of profit will not be too high, but at least Conover's clique will not be taking a cut of it."

"You figure this will hurt Conover?" Barnum asked.

"Indirectly I think it will," Meade said. "If the cattlemen go, I believe I can persuade the Rocky Mountain Lumber Company to break up. With a dozen independent outfits falling, they can form a blockade against Great Northern, which uses a gigantic amount of timber. At this point, I believe Conover can be softened up to the point where we can force him to reveal complete ownership. Once we find that out, we can attack through the courts because I believe that Conover is acting in violation of antitrust legislation."

"That sounds all right," Allendale agreed, and Barnum nodded. "The important thing to remember is that the clique must be broken without destroying the framework of the structure and causing a collapse." He took out a tooled-leather cigar case and passed it around. When everyone had a light, he settled back in his chair and blew smoke at the ceiling. "Regardless of how this is worked, Meade, several of us are going to get hurt and hurt bad. The Silver City Bank will have to go into receivership, as will the Merchants Association, all pending court action and a complete auditing. In the end, I think we will be broke paying off the debts, for all along I have felt that there has been some mighty clever bookkeeping."

Meade grew thoughtful. "Fred, you've put twenty years into the bank. You sure you want to lose it?"

Allendale nodded. "Meade, I'm getting old and not getting anywhere. Maybe I can recover something in the boom that is bound to follow." He got up and crossed to the window, staring out over the darkened land. "There's one consolation, Meade. The land is still here, and the silver will be in the mountains. The sun will still grow grass and animals will eat it." He turned around to face them. "People will build again, and when you're building, you always forget about the last house that fell down."

"What do you get out of this?" Barnum asked. "It seems to me that all you stand to do is lose, Meade."

"That's true," Meade told him. "But like winning, losing is relative. The point is that I will lose a lot less by fighting.

"I need a place to call my camp meeting," Meade added. "Can I have it here, Lige?"

"Why not?" Barnum said. "If you can convince them they should cut their own throats, then I'll throw in with you."

"That's fair enough," Meade said and got up.

He stretched to ease his aching muscles and moved toward the door. "Day after tomorrow," he said, "and thanks, Lige."

"For what? You goin' now?"

"I thought I'd ride over to Hart's," Meade said. "I can make it in two hours."

"Plenty of room here," Barnum murmured.

"I'll feel better being on the move," Meade said and shifted his feet restlessly.

"All right," Barnum said. "Meade, an old man like me is inclined to be nosey, but what about the girl?"

"June?"

Barnum nodded. "This may be something she'll hold against you until her dyin' day. You think of that?"

"Plenty," Meade admitted, and his long lips compressed. "People believe what they want to believe, Lige. If she can't see her way clear now, then she never will. I'm like Fred, Lige—I can lose, too."

"I guess you can," Barnum murmured and watched Meade turn away. The front door slammed, and Meade's boots faded off the porch.

Meade untied the reins and moved around the horse as a man came out of the deeper shadows of the yard. Meade said, "Hello, Pete."

Pete Frame shifted the Winchester from one hand to the other and said, "She's breakin' up, ain't she, Meade?"

Bigelow took his foot from the stirrup and turned to the lanky man. "Do you think so, Pete?"

He nodded. "I've smelled the smoke before, Meade. We had our little disputes in Texas, and it all shapes up. When things are goin' smooth, there ain't no killin's like Hardesty and Clymer. Men stay at home at night with a woman or a bottle. I can smell it plain enough."

"Trouble's easy to find," Meade said and swung into the saddle. "See you," he added and rode from the yard.

From the front window, Barnum watched, and when Meade rode out of sight, he went to the door and beckoned for Pete Frame to come in. The lanky man set his rifle by the door and swept off his hat.

Barnum said, "Saddle a horse, Pete. I want you to go to town."

The man nodded and went out. Crossing to a heavy desk, Barnum took paper and pen and wrote for several minutes. At last he sealed the letter in an envelope and waited until Pete Frame came back.

"Make sure no one sees you," Barnum murmured. "But get this to Amy Falcon. Tell her to see that June Conover gets it."

"Sure," Frame said and stomped off the porch. A moment later he mounted and rode out. Barnum turned back into the house and closed the door.

From his deep chair Allendale said, "That might be a mistake, Lige. Meade might not appreciate it."

Barnum snorted. "I gave away no secrets, Fred. The man's in love with her, and if he knew she was with him, he'd feel better. I'm right. You'll see that I'm right."

"Let's hope you are," Allendale said. "If you're not and Dan sends Garvey after Meade—" He let the rest drift off and rose. "I think I'll start back, Lige. I have a long drive and a slow team."

He took his hat and coat and moved to the door before Barnum spoke. "Fred, do you think he can make it? Breaking Conover, I mean?"

For a thoughtful moment Allendale considered it, then murmured, "No, I don't. But I have to admire his guts."

He went out, and Barnum pulled at his shaggy mustache before going around the room to snuff out the lamps.

Chapter Twelve

After leaving Barnum's headquarters, Meade Bigelow turned east and across the flatness of this valley. Ahead, lesser hills loomed, dark against the lighter night sky. By trotting a mile, then walking one, he began to edge his way up the timbered slopes where his pace slowed.

Fifteen minutes later he came upon the wide logging road and followed its winding path through a deep darkness. The timber grew thick and tall, and a new silence descended.

Far below in the valley, lamplight made a fine pinpoint of light, marking Barnum's place. He and five other ranchers had settled this section of the country. Passing one sawmill, now darkened and odd-looking in the night, Meade urged the horse higher to the wide bench country.

An hour later he came out of the deeper woods and rode through thinning brush and naked stumps. Ahead were the lights of Marilee Hart's company buildings, and Meade gigged the horse into a loose run.

He came into the yard, rode past the jammer and log stack to dismount by a pole corral set up to house the mules. A man came out of a long bunkhouse, and Meade recognized the high shape of Jules Buckley.

Buckley grunted in surprise when he saw Meade, then offered his hand. "I'm surprised," he said, "but glad to see you, Meade."

"Marilee still up?"

"I think so," Buckley murmured. "Trouble, Meade?"

"Lots of it," he said and turned toward the large cabin set against a small rise. At the door, Buckley knocked, and a moment later it opened.

Marilee had a cloth around her head and a robe tight around her. "What?" she said and then saw Meade. "Come in," she murmured and closed the door after them. She touched a taper to three more lamps and indicated chairs.

"Would you like something to drink, Meade?"

"Coffee if it's handy," Meade told her.

"There's always coffee," she said and took cups from a pine cupboard. Meade glanced around the room. Her father had built well, for the walls were finished in varnished pine and the furniture was substantial.

Marilee filled the cups and then took a chair across from them. She saw the day's growth of whiskers on Meade's face and his wrinkled shirt. Meade said, "I *could* use a bath and a shave, couldn't I?"

"What's happening, Meade?" Marilee's voice was even and not at all worried.

"I killed Garroway," Meade said and watched their attention pinpoint. He drank deeply and set the cup aside to explain what had happened at the Great Northern office.

"Conover will be after you for this," Buckley said. "Meade, none of us ever worried about the local law, because Hardesty had only the roughnecks to keep in line. But this is different. Dan will call in a U.S. marshal, and then you're on the run or caught. They don't give up until they get you, and then it's a trial. Even if you got off, you'd be out of the picture and that's what Dan wants."

"My idea is not to get caught," Meade said and lifted his cup again. He explained his visit to Lige Barnum and the proposed meeting of cattlemen for the day after tomorrow. "I figure that I have a little time, Jules. It will be a few days before Dan can get an indictment against me, and after that, I'll take to the hills. Whoever comes after me will have some rough chasing ahead of him."

Buckley nodded and stroked his chin. "We can leave early in the morning," he said. "I think that we can get a meeting together all right. Are you sure that you can sell this thing, Meade?"

"I'm not sure of anything," Meade told him, "except that I've made one mistake right after another and Conover has me where the hair is short. You can see that I have to try, don't you? The only way out of this for me is to cause him so much trouble he'll have to leave me alone."

Marilee stirred and crossed her legs. "Meade,

who do you think is the money behind this?"

"I don't know," Meade said sincerely. "Dan is the Chairman of the Board, and it's my guess that there's a tie-in someplace between the big money and himself. There's no secret about the fact that he owns a large share of Silver City Land and Trust, but not a controlling share. He has complete control of financial disbursement for the combine, but where the money goes and how much is a deep mystery."

"You've been on the board of directors for Great Northern, the same as I have," Buckley said. "That was one of the provisions of the cartel agreement, but I have never yet heard a complete financial report."

"I've gone over the books at Great Northern myself," Meade said, "and something is wrong. The margin of profit and dividends is too small. I've looked for the leak but never been able to find it."

"We're not making any money here," Marilee said. "Under the agreement we own forty-nine per cent in Dad's original mill, and eighteen per cent of the rest. Silver City Land and Trust owns thirty-three per cent to cover prior indebtedness. That's the voting shares because the owners retain only twenty-four per cent of what remains. The other twenty-five per cent, so we are told, is held by Eastern money." She set her cup down and laughed softly. "I'm sorry, Meade. You must be tired. There's a bath house at the end of the crew's quarters, and I imagine Jules will lend you a razor."

Meade got up slowly, favoring his leg. He limped to the door and paused. "Kick me out about six, will you, Jules?"

"The easy life of a big wheel has softened you, Meade. Breakfast is at five-fifteen." Buckley grinned. "I'll have cookie hold something over for you."

"You're a real friend," Meade said and grinned behind his mustache. He closed the door and limped across the yard to the bunkhouse.

As was his habit, Dan Conover ate his supper in the large dining room, but there were long silences between him and his daughter that destroyed any pleasantness connected with the meal.

After Hattie cleared the table, Conover mounted the winding stairs and entered his wife's room. She lay in a massive bed, nearly as pale as the sheets pulled around her throat. He sat down on the edge of the bed and took her frail hand in his.

"My dear, time must be very heavy for you," he said and smiled.

With the immobility of her limbs came feeble interest in living, and she managed to summon a pale smile for him. "I read," she said, "and think. The past can be a beautiful place, Daniel."

"I suppose it can," he murmured and reached

for a cigar, then remembered that she disliked cigar smoke.

"The past can be sad also," she said and looked at him. "You were very handsome when we were married, Daniel. I've never forgotten it."

"A long time ago," he said. "We were very foolish, Bertha."

"Young and foolish," she amended. She laughed ironically. "I tried to kill myself when I found out about that woman in Kansas City." She seized his hand almost desperately. "Did you love her?"

"No," Conover murmured and studied the patchwork design of the bedspread. "She meant nothing to me, Bertha. I never saw her again after the accident.

"Running away solved nothing," Conover said. "You should never have run away, Bertha."

"I know," she said and turned her head away from him to stare at the flowered wall paper. "It's funny, but I never saw her or learned her name. I wanted to, Daniel. I wanted to see her and learn what she had that I lacked. Was my grasp on your love so small?"

"You're tiring yourself," he said and rose. "We've had a good life, Bertha. You must believe that. We've grown strong and big—very big." He leaned forward and kissed her lightly on the forehead. "Try to sleep, my dear."

She didn't turn her head to look at him as he went out and down the stairs.

In the hall he gathered his hat and coat, then paused as June came to the parlor archway. She gave her father a puzzled glance and said, "Business again?"

"It makes the world go round," Conover said dryly and buttoned his coat.

She took his sleeve and held him when he tried to move away. "Are we in trouble, Father?"

"Men with ambition are always in trouble," Conover said and pulled away from her hands. "You'll have to excuse me. I'll be late." She dropped her hands, and he went out. Holding the door open, she watched him go down the walk and turn at the corner, then closed it and went into the parlor, her brows wrinkled with thought.

At the corner of Lode, Conover turned and paced slowly along the walk, nodding pleasantly to acquaintances and miners who were filling the street. At the Trust Company office he paused to insert his key, then lighted a lamp and carried it into the back room. At his desk he sat and wrote a lengthy letter, sealed it, and went back out to the street.

Spotting a man he knew, he called to him, gave him a dollar for a horse, and told him to take the letter to the telegrapher at the mine, who had a small private wire running sixty miles over the mountains and connecting with Denver.

After the man left, Conover extinguished the lamp, locked the office, and walked to the end of the street where the darkness was thickest. He looked left and right, and seeing no one, walked a half block before turning into the alley.

This was a familiar path to him, and he navigated the dark length without incident. Finally, near the other end, he paused and stepped into a narrow gap running between two buildings. This was a tight fit, even for a small man like Dan Conover, but a series of side steps carried him to a door. From an inner pocket, Dan Conover took a key. He inserted it in the lock and stepped inside.

He stood there for a moment listening to the thump of boots on the stairs; then the bead drapes shifted, and Heavy Pearl stepped out, a slow smile lifting her lips.

She touched him and waited, and then he grabbed her roughly and kissed her fervently. When he released her, Heavy Pearl's face held a deeper pleasure, and she lifted her hands to straighten her hair.

Pearl said, "You had me worried, honey."

"You're always worried," Conover murmured and put his arm around her. They went into Heavy Pearl's parlor, and Conover took off his coat and loosened his tie. With his shirt unbuttoned at the throat, he settled into a deep chair, and Pearl took off his shoes, then got his slippers from a closet.

She fixed him a strong drink and handed it to him. Conover watched her and said, "You ought to get yourself some decent clothes. Something that isn't so—"

"What would I do with them?" Pearl asked quickly. "You want too much, Dan. You want me free and easy like I am now, but that's when we're alone. The other times you want me to dress like a swell and ride in a carriage. It's too late for that." She ran her hands through his hair and added, "I've come a long way with you, honey, and all of it's been down." She tipped his head back and kissed him heavily, straining against him. She pulled away and said, "But I'd do it all over again."

"I feel like getting drunk tonight," Conover said and poured himself another drink. "Sometimes I feel like that." He tossed the drink off and then wiped the tears from his eyes.

"What's the matter?" Heavy Pearl asked. "Are you in trouble, Dan?"

He shrugged and tipped up the bottle. "Of course. Predictable trouble I can handle, but there has been a serious slip." He drank half his whisky, then set the glass on the floor. "Because I wanted to get Murray Sinclair, I got careless." He raised his head and looked at Pearl. "Murray has the silver, or at least knows where it is."

"So you were afraid Meade Bigelow would kill Murray," Pearl murmured. "Kill him or join him—either way is bad for you, isn't it?"

"You act like you don't care," Conover said.

"Maybe I don't anymore," Pearl murmured. "I told you that values change, Dan. You should have taken my word for it." She reached down and took the bottle away from him. "You've had enough. If you want to get drunk, do it at home."

He followed her with his eyes as she crossed the room and set the whisky on her dresser. His voice was easy and persuasive. "You're acting strange, Pearl. You getting tired?"

She stiffened, then turned quickly, her face angry. "I want you to stop grabbing, Dan. I want it like it used to be, with none of this sly stuff between us. I don't know what you're thinking anymore."

His smile was thin and somewhat unpleasant. "Does it matter what I think, Pearl? Did it ever really matter?" He shook his head. "Ours was a convenient arrangement. Let's keep it that way."

"I told you I've changed!" Pearl snapped. She saw his smile deepen, and it angered her further. "All right, Dan. Have it your own damn way, but I'm getting fed up. After you leave here, square me up and we'll cut it off. I don't want any more."

This sobered him abruptly, and he shoved himself erect. Crossing the room, he put his arms around her, but she pushed him away.

"Don't do that to me," he said flatly. "By God, I married a woman who screamed on her wedding night because she was afraid of me. I could never get near her until one time I'd had enough and took what I wanted." He clenched his fist and shook it at Pearl. "You slut! Don't you ever say a thing like that to me or push me, you hear?"

For a silent moment Heavy Pearl stared at him. "After all these years I'm just finding out something about you, and it ain't pretty. I've heard about your damn morals that you parade around before people, but I really know you. No wonder your wife screamed. She found out that beneath those lies you were a damned animal, worse than a dog when you got started."

Conover's eyes blazed. "Pearl, I'm warning you!"

"You won't hit me," Pearl said. "Someone will hear the noise and come to see what's going on. You'd rather be dead than have anyone find out about us." She relaxed and sat down in a chair. "I remember the night you brought Jim Hardesty to town, Dan. A big Texas gunfighter. You set him up in the hotel and told Allene Gruen to go to work on him. Only you made a mistake. They fell in love."

"You've said enough!" Dan snapped.

"Not yet," Pearl told him. "Allene came to me early this morning. She said that she told Hardesty that you knew her in Kansas City when she worked for me." She smiled as Conover's mouth opened in shocked surprise. "You think

185

Hardesty won't remember that? What will he do when he does, Dan? Tell Meade?"

"It won't mean anything," Conover said. "There's no crime in a man knowing a woman like that." He moved his thin shoulders restlessly. "I blame this on Murray Sinclair. If the man hadn't been so stubborn in the first place, I would never have had to fire Jim Hardesty or get involved with Meade."

"He'll get you," Pearl said flatly. "You trained him, Dan, and he'll use it against you. Be careful how you play your cards now, because you don't have anything but a busted flush left to play."

"You're sympathetic as hell tonight," Conover said and buttoned his shirt. After tying his string tie, he slipped into his coat and picked up his hat.

"Are you leaving?"

"Why not?" he snapped. "I think you've grown tired of me, Pearl."

"Ah," she said. "That sounds like a tune I know." She intercepted him by the door and put her arm around him. "Stay, honey. I know how to make you forget."

"Some other time," Conover murmured and parted the bead drapes. He let himself out the back door, worked his way through the narrow gap between the buildings, and went down the alley.

When he reached Lode, he paused to give the street a quick sweep with his eyes before stepping out into the stream of traffic. He walked rapidly, dodging the men milling up and down, and when he came abreast of Amy Falcon's Restaurant, he collided with a tall cattleman who had just ducked under the hitchrail.

"Why the hell don't you watch where you're going?" Conover said.

The cattleman straightened and pushed Conover aside. "Grow up before you get sassy to a man, shorty." He walked into the restaurant without a backward glance. For a moment, Conover swayed, half inclined to carry this matter further; then he decided against it and went on down the street.

The cattleman turned just inside the door to see if Conover had followed him, and caught a glimpse as the small man flicked past the large window and was gone.

The counter trade had slacked off, and Amy was in the kitchen washing the last of the dishes. She put her head around the door edge, recognized the man, and said, "Come on back, Pete. I'll give you a piece of pie."

Pete Frame placed his hat on the floor before settling at the table. Amy gave him a quarter of a pie and a fork, and for a moment, Pete focused his attention on eating. When he was through, he said, "Mr. Barnum wanted me to give you this. He says to give it to June when her father ain't around."

He removed his hat and handed her a rumpled letter. Amy took it and held it up to the lamp, turning it over several times. "Why me, Pete?"

The gangly man shrugged. "Don't know. I just follow orders." He scraped his chair back and put on his hat. "Thanks for the pie, Amy. You're real sweet." When Amy looked at him, Pete's face filled with sudden color, and he made a hasty dash toward the front.

Amy smiled when the door slammed. Then her face grew serious, and she went out to the dining room to blow out the lamps and lock the door. Taking her shawl, she left by the back door and traveled the length of the alley to the cross street.

She moved across Lode, then walked along the dirt path until she came to the back street, where she turned left. At Conover's house she knocked, and a moment later Hattie came to the door. The colored woman seemed surprised, but stood aside as Amy stepped into the hall.

"Is Mr. Conover here?"

"No, ma'am," Hattie said. "Miss June is in the study."

"I'd like to speak to her, please."

"I'll see if she's busy," Hattie said and hurried away. Amy waited for a long moment, then heard June's sharp, "No," ring through the house. Laying her shawl on a low bench, Amy moved down the hall and opened the study door.

June whirled quickly and said, "I see you lack not only shame but manners."

"Just a little talk," Amy murmured.

"Please leave us, Hattie," June said, but her attitude was unbending. After the colored woman left, June said, "Please make it brief."

Producing the letter, Amy said, "One of Barnum's riders gave me this tonight. I think it's from Meade."

"I don't want to see it then," June said flatly. "Please get out of the house."

"You are very proud," Amy said, "but it is such a foolish pride."

"Get out," June insisted. "I know that you're in love with him. You've been after him for a long time."

"I wouldn't deny something that's true," Amy told her. "But Meade loves you. Whether I think he's a fool for being in love with you or not is of no importance now. He's in trouble, and he needs you, June. Not many women have an opportunity to stand beside their man. I despise you because you are throwing yours aside."

"I—I don't know whether to believe you or not," June said softly, some of her outrage fading.

"Believe what you want," Amy said. "People always do, but nothing happened, not with Meade, because he has something few men have. Honor."

She turned then and walked into the hall.

She whirled her shawl around her shoulders and opened the door, but June came out of the study and said, "Please. I'm sorry. Can't we be friends?"

"No," Amy said. "Not and both want the same man. Read your letter." She stepped onto the porch, and the door closed behind her. For a moment she felt lost and afraid. But then, she told herself, what else could she have done? He had trusted her to deliver the letter, and she had done as he asked, because she loved him.

At the gate she turned and walked toward her own solitary cabin at the head of the lane. When she lighted the lamp she noticed that the light was without cheer and blew it out before dropping her clothes and getting into bed. The noises of Lode Street filtered through the walls, but she didn't hear them at all.

Chapter Thirteen

For Jean the day began at nine in the evening and carried through to the early-morning hours. She was a small girl, with dark hair and hands that moved nervously when she talked. Once she had been very pretty, but that had been the natural beauty of youth, which had worn away and been replaced by lip rouge and eye shadow.

She was still young, when one measured time in years alone, but beneath a laughing manner lay a complete knowledge of men and the driving urges that brought them to women of her kind. At eleven-thirty there was a lull, and boots no longer tramped up and down the stairs.

Putting on a flowered wrapper, Jean started down to the front parlor. There she gave the slick-haired boy who drummed up trade a dollar and sent him to Karen's Saloon for a bucket of beer. Heavy Pearl came out of her quarters in the back and looked at the litter of cigar butts that had missed the spittoon.

"Men are like hogs," she said and went to the head of the stairs. "Millie! Oh, Millie?" she called, getting a mumbled reply. "Did someone sneak her a bottle?" Pearl didn't wait for her answer, but seized the handrail and hurried up the stairs.

The slick-haired boy came back a few minutes later, and Jean took a water glass and dipped it into the bucket of beer. "Help yourself," she said and the boy beamed as he filled another glass.

Settling back in her chair, Jean tucked her legs beneath her and sipped her beer. Finally she said, "What are you going to be when you grow up, Horace?"

"Gee," Horace said. "I like it here. Do I have to be anything?"

The girl shrugged. "This is no place for you. Why don't you go out and get yourself a decent job? You want men to look down on you?"

"I like it here," Horace insisted, and Jean snorted in disgust. She sipped her beer, raising her eyes when the front door opened and a stubby man came in. He wore a dark pair of pants, a white shirt, and when he took off his coat, black sleeve protectors came to his elbows.

"What's new on the singing wire," Jean murmured and pointed to the bucket of beer. "Have some, Jerry—it's free."

"I will and thanks," Jerry said and filled his glass.

"You're off early tonight," Jean said softly. "Don't you get lonely up there all by yourself?"

He grinned and put his arm around her. "That's why I come to see you," he said, but she pushed him away.

"Things are getting tough," she said in a joking voice. "Next week Pearl is going to charge for looking."

"Next week Silver City is going to come alive," Jerry said and leaned close. "I'll let you in on something, honey. Dan Conover sent to Denver for a U.S. marshal." He gave her a playful punch on the shoulder. "What do you think of that?"

"You're kidding!"

"Sent the wire myself," Jerry insisted.

"What's going on around this town anyway?" Jean asked in an affronted voice. "Bigelow and Hardesty get fired—is the town coming apart at the joints?"

Jerry laughed and let his arm slide around her shoulders. "Who knows what the gods do? What do you say? You busy?"

"Go see Millie," Jean murmured. "She's drunk and will never know the difference."

"You're a card," Jerry said and finished his beer. He winked at her and went up the stairs. When he disappeared along the top hall, Jean untucked her legs.

"Horace," she said softly. "Go get Reilly Sinclair and tell him to hurry."

"Sure," said the slick-haired kid, and Jean sat down again after the front door banged shut. She dipped her glass into the beer again and sat there, waiting with a patience she had learned long ago.

• • •

With breakfast an hour and a half behind them, Meade Bigelow and Jules Buckley rode into Barnum's yard and dismounted. Meade walked with a decided limp, and an increased soreness was running through his leg. During the many miles they had ridden the day before, Meade had been tempted to stop and go back to Marilee Hart's lumber camp, but Buckley was for seeing all the outlying ranchers and Meade stuck it out.

Horses stood along the hitchrail in front of Barnum's house. Buckley said, "Looks like they all showed up." He finished his tie and ducked under the bar while Meade limped around. On the steps, Meade had trouble, for bending his leg proved painful, and he hobbled up to the porch.

In Barnum's large parlor, four heavy-boned cattlemen stood around talking in low, running voices. Barnum saw Meade and came forward, frowning at the big man's pronounced limp.

"You ought to be in bed," Barnum murmured. "How are you, Jules?"

Buckley nodded and moved deeper into the room. Stivers, a cattleman from the valley fringe, put down his drink and shook hands with Buckley. Stivers was a spare man with no non-sense in him.

Raising his hands, Barnum brought an instant quiet and nodded to Meade Bigelow. Meade moved toward the heavy table in the center of the room and sat on the edge to ease his leg.

"Gentlemen," he said, "I believe the last time we were all together in one room was under different circumstances. Great Northern was not an actuality then, but the genesis was there in the newly formed Silver City Land and Trust Company."

Morely, a heavy man from the breaks to the north, spoke up. "Yesterday you didn't go into much detail of what this was all about. What are you figurin' to do, Meade?"

Meade looked at each of them in turn. Wynant was a giant who ruled three thousand acres of bench land. Jorgenson stood against the fireplace, his heavy-boned face expressionless. His blond hair was untidy beneath his hat, and his hands were like hams, hooked into a sagging gunbelt.

"I think all of you are sick to death of being told how much to raise and how much to sell," Meade said. "I can see by the expression on your faces that I haven't missed my guess very far."

"Suppose we are fed up," Wynant said. "You got a sure cure?"

"No one has a sure cure," Meade pointed out and paused to fire up a cigar. "I think that you'll all agree with me when I say that the only reason Silver City Land and Trust ever got you under their thumb was because you were disorganized and fighting among yourselves. All right, you buried the hatchet because you were forced to.

195

By now, the trouble should have died out to the point where you can pull together, but this time, let's pull away from Great Northern interests."

"High finance I know little about," Morely admitted. "Something is explained to me and I understand it or I don't. I'm not making any money and I'll admit it."

"None of you are," Meade said. "There's two sides to this, and I'll explain both of them so that you can't say I hid anything. On the side of organization like the Colorado-Wyoming Cattle Company, which Lige heads, is stability. Morely, we can tell you now how many head you'll be running three years from now, how many you'll keep and how many you'll sell off. We can also tell you who you'll sell to and how much you'll get. Outside prices will not affect you one way or another, because we consume what we produce.

"All that adds up to a very stable economy, with no trouble with your neighbor and a comfortable knowledge of how much money you will make." Meade paused to relieve the ash on his cigar.

"On the other side, the one where each one of you is independent, there will be price fluctuation, depending on the market back East, land and water disputes, and the general crowding that occurs in all cattle countries. But, and this is a very large one, you have the privilege of doing as you damn please, a thing a great many men prize more than life itself."

"I don't understand it," Stivers said bluntly. "You, I mean, Meade. Barnum has told us of the squabble you got in, but why the switch. Ain't you going to marry Mr. Big's daughter?"

"I think that's a dead issue," Meade said. "Not to mention being none of your business anyway."

"Forget I mentioned it," Stivers murmured. "Go on with the talk. You ain't really said nothin' important yet."

"You want both barrels?" Meade looked at each of them. "All right, I want to have an understanding between each of you here and now that all beef sold will be driven to a Denver market and not to Silver City and Great Northern outlets!"

The room was suddenly full of murmuring and shifting of positions. Almost immediately men began to take sides, and Meade let them get going on the subject, then slapped the table for quiet.

"Listen to me," he said and they fell silent. "At first, you will make less trailing to Denver than you will selling to the mines, in town, and the lumber camps, but next year, when you have a herd increase, you'll come out ahead."

"Money always sounded good to me," Morely said, "but I don't want to have Great Northern toughs on my neck. They'll fight over this, won't they?"

"I doubt it," Meade said. "Conover runs Great

Northern, and he's no fool. He won't mix into something he can't win."

"What about the agreement we signed?" Wynant asked. "Seems to me that Great Northern can come in for a cut of our profits."

"Conover would have to collect through the courts," Meade said and rekindled his cigar. "Face the facts. You are in this cartel only because you recognized Great Northern as a ruling company. Now you cease to recognize it and break off relations. How can they collect? Where's the law? We have no courts, except what Great Northern wishes to push as a company policy."

"I don't know," Stivers said. "This is pretty new and sudden and I'd have to think about it."

They murmured their agreement, and Meade turned his head as a horseman pounded into the yard and threw off by the porch. "Go see who that is," Barnum said softly, and Buckley went to the door.

Coming back a moment later, he said, "Reilly, Meade. He wants to talk to you."

"Invite him in," Barnum said, and Buckley went back to the porch. The cattlemen stopped talking as Reilly Sinclair came in, looking uncertain and in a hurry. He crossed over to the table to where Meade sat and said, "Got some news for you. That U.S. marshal Conover sent for arrived this morning."

"So soon?" Meade's brows drew into a furrow. "Murray send you?"

"Yeah," Reilly said. "Sam took Murray in a buggy and headed for the hills. Conover's got a warrant out for you and Murray."

"What about Jim Hardesty?"

Reilly shrugged. "The crowd in Karen's wouldn't go along with the deal that Hardesty drew first, so Conover let it drop."

"I see," Meade murmured and gnawed on his lip. "What kind of guy is this marshal? Tough?"

"He knows what he's doing," Reilly agreed. "Some damn fool wrote June Conover a note and said you was either here or at Hart's. Of course, Childs—that's the marshal—got wind of it and he's headin' here. I'd say that I was an hour ahead of him, maybe a little more."

"I wrote the note," Barnum said and when Meade looked at him, lowered his eyes.

"What the hell did you do that for?" Meade was angry and let it come into his voice.

Barnum shrugged. "I know how you feel about her, Meade. I tried to straighten it out for you. It was just a misunderstanding. She must have told her father."

From the expression on Meade's face, he had more to say. But he waved his hand. "Forget it, Lige. You meant all right." He turned back to Reilly Sinclair. "What do you think?"

"Make yourself damned scarce," Reilly suggested. "Find yourself a spot in the badlands and hole up. Let me know where you're headed, and Hardesty will find you."

Meade nodded in agreement. He looked at the cattlemen, but there was little in their faces to give him hope. He said, "You men don't need me to break this thing. It's up to you to do it. I told you how."

"I don't guess I'd care for it," Stivers murmured. "Sorry to disappoint you, Meade, but buckin' the tiger's for a younger man. I got a family to think of."

"Sure," Meade said and turned his back to them. They filed past him and out of the house. A moment later they were mounted and headed for their own land.

"Meade," Barnum said. "There's a cave up in the badlands in back of Morely's place. The country is rough as hell to get around in. I can make up a pack horse with provisions, and you can lay up there. You ought to get off that damn leg and take care of it."

"I guess you're right," Meade said. "I don't have anything except my bedroll."

"That's not enough up in the high country," Barnum said. "The rains are liable to start any day now. You want to come along, we'll lay out some provisions. Jules, tell Pete Frame to saddle a pack animal and bring him around front."

After Buckley went out, Meade followed

Barnum down the hall and into the kitchen. Barnum gave the cook a quick list, and while the cook sacked the provisions, Barnum gathered other gear together—extra blankets, a lantern, knife, a small hatchet. He tied it all into a large bundle wrapped in a waterproof tarp.

When this was lashed to the pack horse, Meade mounted, shook hands with Barnum and Buckley, then rode out with Reilly Sinclair.

They swung toward the edge of the valley to get into the rocks quickly, and a half hour later pulled up to look down at Barnum's place. There was no sign of life anywhere, and they pressed on.

The day grew warm and they shed their coats, but in the middle of the afternoon clouds began to blot out the sun and they put their coats back on. For the last three hours there had been no sound other than the strike of shod hoofs on rock.

Finally Reilly said, "Meade, what does a man get out of all this?"

"Out of all what?"

"Pushin' Conover out."

Meade smiled. "We don't even know if Conover is the man we want to push, Reilly. He's just Chairman of the Board."

"That's good enough for me," Reilly said. "That son of a bitch has been after us for three years."

"And hasn't caught you yet." Meade grinned. "You worried, Reilly?"

"Maybe," he said. "If this country is turned wide open again, a man might get shot damn easy. Take us for example. We got a good mine, but if it gets to be root, hog, we're liable to end up fightin' for what's already ours."

"But it would be only a few men," Meade pointed out. "Not an organization like Great Northern."

Reilly grunted and fell silent while they crossed a bony ridge and let down into country that was one continuous string of mountains. They followed no trail but clung to natural breaks in the land. Through the afternoon they followed the general direction of the ridges, and when the sun was nearly down, Meade pointed to a cluster of buildings below.

"Morely's," Meade said and turned north.

"You know this place?" Reilly asked.

"Generally," Meade said. "Barnum talked about hunting cats back there."

Reilly turned in the saddle, looking in both directions. "Jesus," he said. "I hope to hell I can find my way out of here. All these damn mountains look the same."

"Just tell Hardesty to stay in the rocks along the ridge until he gets even with Morely's and stay north. I'll be watching for him."

"Sure to hell is wild country," Reilly murmured

and fell silent for the next mile. The trail tilted down, and Meade had a difficult time maintaining his seating with the weight thrown on his bad leg.

They breached a small, sandy-bottomed valley and began to scale the other side. Following openings in the rocks, they worked their way up past stunted brush and tortured-looking trees.

"Bare as a cat's butt," Reilly said. "What the hell can grow here?"

"Nothing," Meade said and stopped to have a look around. Ahead was a table butte, but he could see no trail leading to it. He turned to the left and began to circle. A half mile brought him to a split in the rocks, and he urged his horse through. Reilly followed with the pack horse on a lead rope, and there was barely enough room to clear. The trail was steep and narrow, turning back often, but by the time a full darkness fell, they were in a shallow pocket and ahead was the blacker maw of the cave opening.

Meade dismounted, and Reilly began to unlash the pack. When Meade tried to help, Reilly elbowed him aside and carried the plunder into the cave. Looking around, Meade decided that the rock overhang provided perfect concealment. A fire would never be seen unless someone was in this pocket.

In the daylight the view would be clear for miles and yet give him sufficient cover to hold off anyone who tried to storm the slope. Reilly unlashed the pack and began to hack at the brush with the small ax.

Kindling a small fire, Reilly started the meal, and Meade bent his head to enter the cave, squatting along one wall. This was not a big place, but it was ten feet deep and nearly that wide. A fire at the mouth would provide plenty of heat.

After their meal, Reilly stretched out on his blankets and rested his head on his folded hands. "This is easy money," he said and went to sleep.

Meade watched the fire until it died to red coals, then lay down. His leg throbbed and he worried it around, trying to find a comfortable position. Somewhere in the process sleep claimed him.

Chapter Fourteen

When Reilly Sinclair rode into Silver City it was noon and the whistles were blowing at the mine. On the hotel porch, Hardesty sat with his feet elevated, watching the thin traffic move up and down Lode Street. As Reilly passed at a walk, he gave Hardesty a deliberate glance, then raised his eyes briefly to the room above, a signal that Hardesty clearly understood.

After dismounting across the street, Reilly went into the saloon, and Hardesty left his chair and entered the hotel lobby. Taking the stairs, he went down the hall and into his room.

He sat by the window and waited until Reilly came from the saloon and sauntered across the street. A fresh wind lifted dust and pelted it along in a tawny cloud, and a moment later, boots sounded on the stairs and Hardesty's door opened.

"Where's that damned marshal?" Reilly asked.

"Up at the mine with Conover," Hardesty said. "Some kind of conference."

Reilly sagged against the wall and fashioned a smoke. "Got Meade holed up," he said. "You know the badlands above Morely's place?"

"Generally."

Reilly grunted and gave Hardesty the general directions. "Think you can find it?"

"I'll find it," Hardesty murmured. "You better get out of town. You took a hell of a chance coming here in broad daylight."

"I'm not worried about that marshal," Reilly said.

"Better be," Hardesty warned. "He's a determined cuss, so watch yourself. When he came back from Barnum's yesterday, he wasn't disappointed. He just figured there'd be another day."

"I'll use the back stairs," Reilly stated and moved toward the door. "From now on, I'll leave it to you to contact Meade. He'll be watching for you." Reilly opened the door, gave the hall a quick glance, then stepped out, closing the door behind him.

After waiting a decent interval, Hardesty rolled his coat and went downstairs. He saw no sign of the marshal on the street and decided that Childs wasn't back from the mine yet. At the stable, he saddled his horse, and the stableman came back for the latest gossip.

"Goin' someplace?"

Hardesty shot him a glance that told him to mind his own business, but the man pushed it aside. "You was damned lucky you had witnesses," he said. "Clymer had friends in Silver City."

Hardesty lashed his coat behind the cantle and put a foot in the stirrup. The stableman took his sleeve and held him for a moment. "Them Sinclairs ain't goin' to last long with the marshal after 'em. Your friend Meade, either. You hear that Garvey turned up missin'?"

Hardesty's attention sharpened. "What do you mean?"

The old man moved his shoulders. "Just missin', that's all. He left the mine, ridin' toward town, but he never got here. Never got back to the mine either. That's what the marshal's so hot about this morning."

"That's real interestin'," Hardesty murmured and swung his leg up and over. He turned the horse toward the stable arch and walked him slowly down Lode.

At the end he paused and sat lazy in the saddle, for ahead of him, Childs rode toward him at an easy lope. The marshal pulled his horse up, and his eyes flicked over Hardesty quickly, but did not miss a thing.

Childs was not a big man, neither was he impressive until a man looked into his eyes. They were a deep brown and wide-spaced, but in their chocolate depths a great courage flowed. He wore a dark suit and flat-crowned hat, and beneath his coat, a short-barreled .45 sat high against his hip.

He said, "Traveling, Hardesty?"

"I move around a lot," Hardesty murmured. "I'm the restless type."

"Sure," Childs murmured and licked a cigar

into shape. "One of these days you're going to catch up with yourself. Then where are you going to be?"

"I'm not running from anything," Hardesty said flatly.

"That's right," Childs agreed. "You're smart, Jim. Every shootin' you ever been involved in has been out in the open where people could see it. One of these days you're going to push your luck a little too far."

"The lecture over?" Hardesty asked.

Childs waved his hand. "Go on—but when you see Meade Bigelow, tell him that this warrant I carry for him don't get cold. I'll be after him, and I'll find him."

"Who said I was goin' to Meade?"

Childs laughed softly. "Hardesty, I just look dumb." He lifted the reins and moved on, and Hardesty turned in the saddle to watch the marshal ride down the street.

Childs dismounted in front of Amy Falcon's restaurant, then went inside. One man sat alone at the long counter, and when he saw the marshal, finished his meal, laid his fifty cents down, and hurried out.

Ralphie stacked dishes, and Amy came from the back room. She saw Childs and said, "Take an hour off now, Ralphie." After the boy left, she murmured, "Something to eat?"

"Whatever you have," Childs said and laid his

hat on the counter. He was not a young man—she guessed his age at forty—but he smiled easily and there was something pleasant in his blunt face.

She fixed him a steak, with potatoes and stewed tomatoes, topping it off with pie and coffee. While he ate, she went to the front door, locked it, and hung a sign: *Closed.* Childs turned his head to watch this and smiled, but said nothing.

Amy went behind the counter and stood facing him, her arms crossed over her ample breasts. Childs finished his meal and lifted his coffee cup. "You don't seem worried," he said.

"What have I to worry about?" She did not pretend not to know what he was talking about. "Meade can take care of himself. Besides, he didn't murder Garroway."

His lip ends pulled down in a shrug. "Cord Butram and Garvey were there. They saw it."

"Garvey is missing," Amy said softly. "That leaves Cord's word against Meade's, doesn't it?"

"We wouldn't want anything to happen to Garvey, miss. That could come back and hit Bigelow right between the eyes." He took a cigar from his pocket, nibbled at the end, then arced a match. "Hardesty left town. Probably going to Meade right now."

"I saw him," Amy said. "Childs, you're a fool! Can't you see what's happening? Conover is piling this on Meade because he wants to get rid of him!"

"Can't say as I blame him," Childs said. "Seems to me he's gone wild, killing a man, inciting Barnum to revolt against a legal corporation. He's your man, maybe you can tell me what got into him."

"He's not my man," Amy said flatly. "If you want to pump somebody, go see June Conover."

"I don't pump anybody," Childs said and knocked ashes into his coffee cup. "The trouble with most men is they want to do everything in a day." He shook his head. "Not me. As far as I'm concerned, Meade broke the law and I'll catch him. He'll get a trial, and then he can say his piece. I'll get Murray Sinclair, too."

"You *are* a fool," Amy snapped. "Childs, your case against Murray will not stand up in court."

"That's not my problem," he murmured. "Warrant says they're wanted. That's all I go by." Childs slid off the stool and laid a half dollar on the counter. "It's been a pleasant talk," he said, "but I'd advise you not to interfere."

"That's your lookout," Amy told him and went around the counter to open the door. After he went back to the street, she reversed the sign and walked to the kitchen. Once away from prying eyes, she dropped her mask and let her worry show.

Darkness was creeping into the street, laying shadows along the building walls, when Jim Hardesty returned to town. He rode down the middle of the street and dismounted in front of Gruen's hotel.

Conover and his daughter were leaving the Silver City Land and Trust Company office, and Hardesty paused, lifting his hat to June as she went by on her father's arm. Dan Conover grunted a brief greeting, but gave Hardesty no more than an aloof glance.

Amy watched this from the front window, turning away when Jim Hardesty entered the hotel. For an hour she cleaned the kitchen, blackening the stove and straightening the pots and pans hanging from wall brackets. Ralphie came back after seven, and Amy locked the door, putting him to work scrubbing the kitchen floor.

She watched the street, and at eight, saw June Conover come down the street and enter the hotel. Amy Falcon turned away then, for the watching and waiting was over. She had no further part in this.

In the lobby, June glanced around, then went up the stairs. At Allene's door she knocked and was admitted. She stopped suddenly when Jim Hardesty lifted his eyes and gave her an unfriendly stare.

Allene said, "Sit down, June. You look upset."

She sank into a chair and stripped off her gloves. She wore a long dress, tight at the collar and sleeves. Giving Hardesty a frank glance, she said, "You saw him, didn't you?"

"I didn't see anything," Hardesty said flatly. "I went elk hunting."

"Is Meade all right?" June said, leaning forward slightly. "Please, can't you see that I have to know?"

Hardesty glanced at Allene Gruen, but she turned away, offering no advice. He said, "What do you have to know?"

"I—we quarreled. It was a stupid, silly thing, and I shouldn't have believed what I did." She spread her hands appealingly. "Lige Barnum wrote me a note. I believed it, because I don't think I ever stopped loving Meade. Can't you see that? Why would I have come here like this if I didn't?"

Hardesty pawed his mouth out of shape and sat there, fingering his mustache. "What do you want me to do about it?"

"I have to see him," June said quickly. "Please, take me with you when you go to him again."

"That's a crazy notion you have," Hardesty said. He shook his head. "Better forget it. Meade's got enough trouble without adding you to the pile."

June turned her argument on Allene. "Mrs. Gruen, you understand, don't you. Can't you convince him for me?"

"It's not my affair," Allene said bluntly. "If you hadn't been such a fool in the first place, you wouldn't be worrying about it."

"I know I was wrong," June said and appeared on the verge of tears. "Please, don't I deserve this chance?"

Allene's face was thoughtful, and she said softly, "Can you take her without being followed?"

"No," Hardesty said flatly. "Sorry, Miss Conover, but you'll have to do without."

She stared at Hardesty for a moment, then stood up, her skirts rustling faintly. "I see. You don't trust me, is that it?"

"Let's just say I can't take a chance with you."

June turned to the door and went out quickly. She hurried down the stairs and paused when she entered the lobby. Amy Falcon rose from a deep chair and crossed to her. June said, "Go ahead and try if you want, but he won't take you either."

"It's not my place to go," Amy said softly. "I was afraid that Hardesty would be a fool, though, and take you."

June's lips turned unpleasant. "You hate me, don't you?"

"No. I just think Meade is settling for pretty cheap merchandise."

"Oh!" June said, her eyes round with shocked surprise. She whirled suddenly and ran from the hotel.

Men moved along the street, and a stiff wind lifted dust, whipping it against the buildings in a stinging spray. Her voluminous skirts billowed against her legs and made walking difficult. With her head down, she hurried on, crying out in surprise when the red end of a cigar glowed from a gap between two buildings.

Childs said, "You'd tell me if you knew where he was, wouldn't you?"

June hurried on without answering him. At the corner she turned on the side street and hugged the dark buildings that acted as a windbreak. On the other corner she turned again, and a few minutes later was on her own porch and ringing for Hattie.

In the hall, she paused to remove her hat, and her father came from his study, shrugging into his coat. He gave her an irritated glance, but said nothing. He went out, and June listened as his footsteps faded down the path.

Dan Conover did not go near Lode Street, but stayed in the residential section. At a large house one street over, he turned at the gate and rattled a brass knocker. Fred Allendale answered the door and motioned for Conover to come in, then took the man's hat and coat.

Allendale ushered Conover into the parlor, where a fire crackled in the fireplace. The wind rattled a loose shutter in the back of the house.

"Blowing pretty fair," Allendale said and offered brandy. He waited until Conover was settled with his glass, then said, "Something on your mind, Dan?"

"A little business deal," Conover murmured. "I think we can both stand to make a profit from it."

"I've lost interest in making money," Allendale said smoothly and lifted his brandy. "We're getting old, Dan. Time to retire and let someone else have the game."

"Those are my sentiments exactly," Conover said. "Fred, I don't feel like getting involved in this mess with Meade Bigelow and Murray Sinclair. They've stepped outside the law now, and I'm content to let the marshal handle them. Frankly, I own a lively interest in the Silver City Land and Trust Company, your bank, and the Merchants Association. I want to liquidate my holdings, Fred. I can make you a proposition you can't afford to turn down."

Allendale's brows wrinkled and he gave it a long study, before speaking. "A transfer?"

"I was thinking of something like that," Conover murmured. "Frankly, Fred, I'm a little shy of ready cash and I found something else that looks good." He laughed easily and refilled his brandy glass. "The chairmanship of Great Northern is getting to be too much for me. I own the voting block in Silver City Trust, a quarter of the Consolidated Merchants, and a quarter of the bank. By making a transfer, I'll assume your quarter shares in the bank and merchants, and you can take over the Silver City Land and Trust. Also the chairmanship of Great Northern."

"What about the other shareholders?" Allendale asked. "Surely they will have something to say about such a drastic policy change."

"I can control them," Conover assured him. "For some time now I've been wanting to move into a smaller field."

Allendale shook his head. In the hall, the tall clock chimed softly and he rose to throw another chunk of wood on the fire. For several minutes he paced up and down the room, then stopped and said, "I don't think I want it, Dan."

"Why not?" Conover asked. "I'm stepping down. Doesn't that please you?"

"Would you consent to a complete audit of the books?"

Conover laughed. "We're as sound as a dollar, Fred. You're not worried about that, are you?"

"You're too sound," Allendale said bluntly. "Frankly, I've always questioned the profit margin of Great Northern and associated cartels. To my way of thinking the glutton's share has been channeled through the trust company and into someone's pocket. Maybe yours, Dan."

Conover was on his feet, his face flushed and angry. "Damn you, Fred, I don't have to take talk like that!"

"You'll take it from me," Allendale said. "Dan, I think you're getting ready to abandon ship if things go wrong. Personally, I doubt whether Great Northern could survive an auditing. The company is operating on a shoestring while your pockets, or someone's pockets, are bulging with mischanneled funds." Allendale moved toward the door and handed Conover his coat and hat. "Now get out of my house."

"Very well," Conover said and stepped out the door. "You're just a little man, Allendale. Remember that I can swallow you whole any time I want to."

"Be the roughest meal you ever had," Allendale said and closed the door.

Going down the path to the road, Dan Conover stumbled, for his rage was so great that he was almost blinded by it. Through a series of maneuvers along the back streets, he entered the gap between two buildings and inserted his key in the lock.

Closing the door behind him, he heard the spring lock snap and parted the bead drapes. Heavy Pearl was in a pink lounging robe that showed her full figure, and Conover threw his hat in the corner.

"I thought you'd be back," Pearl said and smiled. "It may not be love anymore, but the habit's there."

"Don't talk filth!" he snapped and poured himself a drink.

She watched him toss it off and said, "Worried?"

"It's time to go somewhere else, Pearl. The hounds will be closing in soon."

"That shouldn't worry you," she said and stood up, stretching. "They've closed in before, and you never got caught."

"This is different," Conover said and took another drink. "This is *big,* Pearl—bigger than anything I've ever handled." He sat down and mopped a hand across his face. "When everything was running smoothly, the loose ends didn't matter, because they lay flat and no one noticed them, but now there's a wind blowing and they're flying all over hell. I feel like a kid trying to catch the wiggling end of a kite before it blows away."

"Some kids lose their kites," Pearl said, and from her tone he understood that she didn't care one way or another.

"This kite I want to hang on to," he said. "It's not like that business in Kansas City when I made Ellington the big shot and let him sign everything. When the law moved in, they grabbed him and had nothing on me. Here I'm implicated up to my neck."

For a moment she grew very quiet, then asked, "How much did you steal this time, Dan?"

He looked at her for a moment, but there was nothing on her face that gave him hope. "A cool million," he said and watched her shrug and turn away, only remotely interested.

"Well," she said, "you never were a piker in anything."

"Is that all you have to say, Pearl?"

Her shoulders rose and fell. "What more is there to say, Dan? You've always made your own rules. One slick deal after another. A man can outsmart himself sometimes."

"Thanks for the sympathy," he said sarcastically.

"I've run out of sympathy. I've run out of everything." She faced him again. "Dan, I want to settle up. I mean it!"

"You're getting alarmed over nothing," he said and started to get up, but the look in her eyes stopped him halfway.

"Do you think I'm fooling?" Her lips pulled tight against her teeth, and her eyes were as hard as his. "I either get it or I go to your wife. I've got a lot to tell her, Dan. When I get through, you won't be able to walk down the street."

He sagged back in the chair, and a film of perspiration glistened on his cheeks. "Pearl, honey—" he began, then shook his head.

"You were so smart!" Pearl snapped. "I told you to leave Murray alone, that he'd cause trouble. When he took that silver away from Clymer and Garvey, he had you by the tail, but you didn't have enough sense to quit pushing him. You never should have given Meade that phony report about Garvey seeing Murray. Sure, you wanted Murray taken care of, but you picked the wrong man to do it, Dan. Meade Bigelow is honest, and that was your mistake. You should have sent Clymer after Murray, not an honest man. You got the wildcat by the tail now, wanting Meade caught, but afraid what he'll say if he is. It don't take much now, Dan, because once the ball gets rolling, they'll pick at you until they find you out. You better get out now."

"No!" he said. "There's a way. I hate it, but there is one way to buy time." He left the chair and retrieved his hat. "Stay with me, Pearl. Stay with me."

"Why not?" she asked. "Habit works both ways, don't it?"

Chapter Fifteen

Waiting was a tedious task to Meade Bigelow, and he found the solitude of the cave almost unbearable after the first day. By picking his way carefully through the rocks, he roamed into the badlands toward Morely's place, and at noon of the second day, hunkered down in a fissure to survey the valley floor.

His leg still bothered him, but he had lanced it the night before and some of the swelling had gone down. A stiff wind tore across the land, booming among the rocks, and he pulled his coat tighter around his neck to keep out the sharp bite.

Along the fringe of the badlands, a solitary rider moved toward Meade's place of hiding. Meade waited. An hour dragged by, and finally he recognized Jim Hardesty on a livery roan. When Hardesty was yet a half mile off, Meade pitched a rock down the slope and it built into a small slide of loose stones.

This drew Hardesty's attention, and he looked up. Meade waved, and the ex-marshal altered his course. His horse was blowing from the climb, and Hardesty dismounted to hunker down beside Meade.

"That marshal still after me?" Meade asked.

Hardesty nodded. "He won't give up." After

rolling and lighting a cigaret, he added, "Something's happened that I don't understand. Dan Conover closed Great Northern. Everything's at a standstill, stores, bank, freight wagons—the whole caboodle."

"Son of a bitch," Meade said softly. "He's playing this so damned smart."

"Sure don't follow you," Hardesty murmured and drew deeply on his smoke. He looked at the kicked-up dust. "Going to blow up a heller pretty soon." He threw his cigaret away. "Can Conover put the lid on Great Northern like that?"

"Sure," Meade said. "He's Chairman of the Board, and if he feels the organization is shaky, he can suspend operations for a specified period of time. That means that there will be nothing stirring anyplace. No money going in or out until a group of auditors are appointed by the court and go over the books."

"Christ," Hardesty said. "How long will that take?"

Meade shrugged. "Conover will have to contact the principal shareholders back East and get some friendly judge to appoint an accountant. May take a month."

"Silver City will blow away in a month," Hardesty said. "What does a move like that mean, Meade?"

"Don't know for sure," Meade admitted. "A lot of things. The organization may be going on the rocks, but I doubt it. He could do this to panic the stockholders and kick the props out of the market, then buy it all up at a fraction of the cost."

"Sure wish you was back in town, Meade." Hardesty stood up and rubbed his flat stomach. "I'd better be getting back. I almost forgot, but Garvey has turned up missing. No one has seen him for a couple of days."

"You seen Reilly or Sam?"

"Haven't been near their place," he admitted. "Childs was snoopin' around their claim, but they were gone. Lit out someplace."

Hardesty moved toward his horse and swung up. Meade followed him to the off stirrup and said, "A few more days up here and I'll go crazy."

"You go crazy then," Hardesty murmured. "Childs won't give up until he has you, Meade. He's a determined bugger."

"I'm not doing any good running."

"You'll do less in jail," Hardesty said. He leaned on the saddlehorn and crossed his wrists. "Seems to me that if Conover was aimin' to bust you and Murray and me up, he sure as hell did a good job of it without raisin' a sweat." He grinned. "See you around, Meade," he said and urged the horse into motion.

Meade watched him for better than an hour and then lost interest. Rising from his belly-flat position, he turned to get his horse, then stopped, for below in the rocks, a man picked his way carefully. Switching his glance, Meade saw Hardesty out on the flats, moving away, and cursed, for he had already guessed that the man coming toward him was Childs.

He changed position carefully and began to work to a lower level, cautiously stepping to avoid loose rocks that would roll and betray his position. Twenty minutes of this brought him to a narrow split, a natural defile through which the man must pass.

Meade lay down to wait, his short-barreled .44 ready.

To a man in his position, it seemed that hours passed before he heard a step and the fast breathing, then a heartbeat later, the figure passed ten feet below him. Meade said, "Hold it right there!"

With a small shriek, June Conover stumbled, and her hat fell off, allowing her hair to tumble over her shoulders. For a surprised moment, Meade remained motionless, then hurried down to her level, ignoring the sharp pain in his leg.

She touched him, then threw her arms around him and began to cry. "Meade," she said between sobs. "I lost Hardesty. I thought I would never find you."

With his arm around her he led her to the shelter of a large slab rock where the wind was less biting. There he knelt down and held her until she stopped crying.

"I've been so worried about you," she said. "Meade, I was such a fool. I've never stopped loving you, regardless of everything."

For a moment he felt a sharp resentment, but this passed and he smiled. "I'm glad you came, June, but you have to leave."

"But I want to be with you," she said hotly. "Meade, please give yourself up and come back with me. You'll never prove your innocence by hiding."

"I hate to say this, but your father would be the first to whip the horse out from under me." Meade shook his head. "Right now I have a mighty poor hand to play, June, but it might pick up. Jim said Dan closed the mines and everything else. What's going on, June?"

"He never tells me anything," she said quickly. "Lately he's been acting so strange and drawn. He's hardly ever home."

Drawing a deep breath, Meade said, "Honey, I've never asked you anything about the Silver City Trust Company books, but I'm going to now. I know that Great Northern pays all monies to the Trust Company, but where do the checks go? Who collects on the other end?"

"People back East," June said. "I thought you knew that, Meade. There's a bank in St. Paul. One in Detroit. Another in Kansas City, and the

Metropolitan Trust Company of Baltimore."

"They are the other stockholders?"

"Why of course, Meade." She laughed softly. "I know that you've always had a dream of some monster sitting in a room full of money taking all the profits from Great Northern, but that isn't so. These companies are made up of a lot of little people who put in small amounts. Father has told you that time and time again."

"Sure," Meade murmured. "And I used to believe it, but now I don't. When I was a kid we used to play a game where we hid something. I can remember that one kid always hid his the best because he made a lot of motions and lost the article under the cover of this activity. A thing like this goes on and on, June, until the real ownership is lost."

"Why do you hate my father so much, Meade? Did it come on so suddenly?"

"I guess not," he admitted. "A thing like that creeps up on a man, and then he thinks it. I believe I said it for the first time the night I had my trouble with Murray Sinclair. Then I knew that your father was a dishonest man."

She grew silent and studied her folded hands. "That's not nice to hear."

"Sorry," Meade said. "I think it's a fact, not an opinion."

She put her arms around him and pillowed her head against his chest. "I've been lost without you," she said softly. "Kiss me, Meade. Show me that you love me."

When she raised her lips, he kissed her and tried to summon a fervency to answer her own, but there was none and the shock left him bewildered. She sensed this change and released him. "Can't we go someplace else?" she asked.

"Run?"

"What's wrong with running?" She raised a hand to his unshaven cheek. "This isn't your country, darling. Let Father have it if he wants it. Why do you want to fight when you can't win?"

"By not fighting I can lose my self-respect," he said.

"Men put much store by that, don't they?"

"To some men that's all there is left," Meade said and shifted to a more comfortable position. "You better go back, June. There's a storm in the making."

"Would I shock you if I said I wanted to stay? Meade, I mean it!"

He pushed her away from him and stood up. "You're talking cheap," he said, and his voice was hard. Taking her by the arms, he lifted her. "This isn't your way, June. You're lying and doing it badly." He dropped his hands away from her and stood quietly.

"I'm not very good at pretending at that, am I?" She touched him fleetingly, then let her hand slide away. "Being honest, I didn't want to come here, but I owed that to you, Meade." She gave a short, nervous laugh. "I'm afraid that my love is the drawing-room kind. Are you offended, Meade?"

She focused her eyes on his and watched his displeasure thaw. At the proper moment she kissed him lightly and said, "I'll go back because I really want to, but I do love you, Meade. Do you believe that?"

"I don't know," he said and looked at her, but didn't touch her.

When Homer Childs was a boy on the Kansas prairies, he learned to hunt birds with a .22 rifle, and the lessons mastered had stood him in good stead through eighteen years of man-hunting. He worked slowly and with great care and never got excited when the quarry was about to be flushed. And now, he felt an old familiar sense of contentment come over him, for he was about to flush his game one more time.

Through the day he watched the people move around Silver City's streets, and soon Homer Childs began to feel the pattern of this town. When Conover closed the Great Northern, the huge machine that controlled this land plowed to a sluggish standstill, but this had no effect on Childs.

He was busy watching a girl, and when Jim Hardesty saddled his horse and rode from town,

228

Childs did not leap into the saddle to follow him. He waited until he saw June Conover, clad in a pair of man's jeans and a blue work shirt, leave, then went to the stable to leisurely saddle his own mount.

Tracking was not difficult for Childs knew that Bigelow was in the badlands. He knew and didn't care, for he understood men and realized that hiding was alien to their nature and sooner or later they would tire of it and come back for another look at the town.

The girl presented an easy trail, although she stayed in the rocks and out of sight. Once he had her general direction, he needed little else to guide him. Occasionally he would pause high in the rocks and sweep the valley with his eyes. Twice during the day he picked up the small figure of Jim Hardesty below, and when Hardesty turned and began to climb, Childs stopped, for his quarry was in easy grasp.

He watched and waited and saw Hardesty leave. Another hour passed and the wind buffeted him, but still he clung to his place in the rocks. Darkness was not far off now, and Childs wished that it would hurry, because it covered many things and he needed that cover.

At last he moved out, leading his horse. By moving carefully, he let the wind drown out any noise that he made, and within an hour, knew he was in the vicinity of Bigelow's hiding place.

Picketing his horse, Childs began a systematic search afoot. With what light remained, he studied the land below him, and when he saw a flicker of movement, eased his way down.

A few minutes later he heard the run of their voices, distorted by the wind, and drew his gun. Bigelow was leaning against a slab-shaped rock, a half-smoked cigaret in his fingers. The girl was by his side, lying on her back, with one arm flung over her face.

Homer Childs said, "I have you covered, Bigelow. You're under arrest."

Slowly Meade raised his eyes to the man who stood ahead of him, braced against a split in two rocks. The gun in Childs's hand was steady, and he jumped down. June sat up quickly and began to cry.

"No need for that," Childs murmured. "If you have a horse, miss, I'd advise you to get on it and get back to town."

She looked like she was going to argue, and Meade slipped his voice in. "Go on, June. The hiding's over now."

"Good-by," she said and turned away, moving down the rocky slope toward a spot where she had hid her horse.

"Where's your horse?" Childs asked.

"Twenty yards up the hillside," Meade said. He stood up then, and Childs became cautious.

"Turn around and put your hands over your

head. Now lean against that rock." When Meade obeyed, Childs reached around him and slipped the gun from Meade's holster. He patted Meade's pockets and found nothing.

"We'll go up and get your horse now," Childs said and stayed behind Meade as he inched his way up the steep slope. "Your leg bothering you some?"

"Some," Meade said and did not speak again until he was mounted.

The smell of rain was clear in the whipping wind, and the clouds were lower now. Childs made Meade go ahead, giving directions in a curt voice until they came to the spot where he had picketed his own horse. Mounting, Childs said, "We'll move down a ways to where there's some timber and spend the night."

He said nothing more, and Meade picked his way out of the rocks. A thick darkness had settled over the land and the traveling was slow, but finally Childs selected a sheltered campsite and ordered Meade to dismount.

From his saddlebags, Childs took bacon and coffee, along with a small skillet and coffee-pot. He squatted by the growing blaze he kindled and shaved bacon into the pan, while Meade gathered wood.

"Are you going to behave yourself?" Childs asked.

"I haven't made up my mind yet," Meade said.

"I can put a pair of handcuffs on you until you do," Childs told him. He slanted a glance toward Meade. "You went wild all of a sudden, didn't you? Want to tell me about it?"

"There's nothing to tell," Meade said flatly. "I shot Garroway in self-defense. He and Garvey were holding me while Cord Butram put a head on me. I broke away, hit back, then shot Garroway when he tried to draw."

"Garvey's disappeared," Childs murmured. "So's the Sinclairs. Looks like you're holding the sack, Bigelow."

"Who cares," Meade said and stared at the fire. "Conover played his ace when he closed Great Northern. I can't top that."

"Better forget it," Childs suggested. "The best thing for you to do is get a lawyer and let him do the figuring. There's a tin plate in the saddlebag. I'll use the skillet."

They ate in silence, and the bacon took the sharp edge off Meade's appetite. He took the coffee-pot from Childs, took a drink, and handed it back. Between them, they passed it back and forth until it was empty. Meade sat back while Childs cleaned the skillet with dirt.

Rising, Childs took a pair of handcuffs from his back pocket and tossed them in Meade's lap. "Those ought to fit. Put 'em on."

For a moment Meade stared at them, then clamped them around his wrists, drawing the crescents down until the ratchets stopped clicking. He didn't like the feel of them, cold and unyielding. His emotions broke through his control, and he fought them for a savage moment and in the end, sat back, shaking and sweating.

Childs, who watched everything so carefully, said, "Never been in trouble before, have you?"

"No."

"Garroway the first man you ever killed?"

Meade nodded.

"Let's get some sleep," Childs suggested and unrolled his blankets. The marshal unsaddled his horse and gave Meade the blanket, which was not enough, but better than nothing. The thick, woolly clouds blotted out the night light, and the wind tore through the foliage.

Sleep would not come to Meade, and around midnight he sat up. The fire was nearly dead; only one solitary coal glowed redly. Childs stirred, awake and cautious.

"Go to sleep," he said, and Meade lay back down, trying to draw warmth from the blanket. The wind picked up in strength, moaning as it whipped through the trees. The first splatter of rain hit Meade in the face, and he sat up again. Childs threw aside his blankets and took an oilskin from his saddleroll. He lay down and rolled in it.

Rain began to fall harder, then steadied to a downpour. There was no more thought of sleep for Meade, and he got up, gathering wood to rekindle the fire.

"What the hell are you going to do now?" Childs asked.

"If I can't keep dry, at least I can keep one side warm," Meade said and fanned the small blaze, adding wood until it leaped high. He squatted before it, feeding it until he was forced to back up. The brightness drove the night back, and he felt less lonely.

He listened to the wind slash and whine and the whisper of the slanting rain as it pelted the trees. The water hissed and snapped in the fire, and he failed completely to hear the horse approach; the slash of water in the trees drowned out all sounds.

The first inkling that another person was standing at the outer edge of light startled him as much as it did Childs, who threw back his blanket with a rush, then froze.

Amy Falcon's eyes glowed over the octagon barrel of her rifle. Her golden hair was hanging in soaked ropes over her shoulders. Her skin was slick with rain and had a metallic sheen to it in the fire's dancing flicker.

"Get his gun and yours, Meade."

"You can't get away with this," Childs said, but made no move for his gun as Meade relieved him of both of them. He glanced at Amy and said softly, "I had you pegged as his woman from the beginning."

"I'll have to drive off your horse," Meade told Childs.

"Don't go on the dodge," Childs said. "If you're innocent you'll be set free, Meade. The law's fair."

"When Dan Conover leaves the scales alone it is," Amy said, still covering Childs with the rifle. "Unlock the handcuffs, Marshal, and don't try to be a hero." She waited while Childs produced the key and the handcuffs dropped to the ground.

Taking Childs's cartridge belt and holstered gun, Meade buckled it around his waist; he replaced his own gun in his shoulder holster. Amy picked up a stick and shied it at Childs's horse, then listened while it ran off in the night.

"Sorry about this," Meade said and whirled, leaving the ring of firelight. He limped badly when he tried to hurry, and the second try put him up on his horse.

For an hour they threaded their way through the pelting rain, and then Meade edged to the right and began angling up a faint trail leading to the higher, rock-studded slopes. She followed him without question although he was heading for the badlands where Childs had picked him up.

Daylight was not far off when Meade came to a large fissure and urged his horse through. Passing this stone archway, he began a series of switchbacks as the trail climbed steeply. At last he came to the hollowed-out depression, and now there was enough light to outline the black maw of the cave.

He picketed the horses and pushed her ahead of him. She squatted against one wall, shivering, for she was soaked to the skin. She wore a faded pair of jeans, a man's shirt, and a frayed corduroy coat. The night chill was heavy, and her teeth were chattering.

"I'll get a fire going," Meade said, and his hands shook as he broke dead branches. After three tries he managed to strike a match and blew on the feeble flame, watching it catch. When it grew a foot high, he added more branches until it threw out a thick heat.

Crowding close to the fire, Amy absorbed enough of the heat to warm her, and her teeth stopped chattering. Her clothing began to steam. "Turn your back to me," she said and took off her coat and shirt. Standing, she slipped out of her jeans and squatted close to the blaze, clad only in a wet shift that came barely to her knees. Her shoulders and arms were bare, and she turned so that the heat struck her squarely.

Meade got her a blanket and wrapped her in it, then made a rack of sticks to dry her clothes on. Her jeans were thin and dried quickly, and she stood up to slip into them.

"Did you follow Childs?" She nodded. "He followed June."

"Hardesty told her that he wouldn't take her,"

Amy said. "She's a stubborn fool, and I had an idea that Childs would follow her."

He sat there before the fire, his shirt hung on the branches to dry. Dancing light flickered against his skin, and he began to massage his sore leg.

"Still hurting you?" She moved around, throwing the blanket aside. "You'll lose your leg if you're not careful." Her voice was full of concern, and he raised his eyes to hers. Her glance held him like a pair of strong arms. Many times before he had wondered what it meant, and now it became clear in that moment. The knowledge of her feeling shocked him, excited him, pleased him beyond his power to describe. Even after he pulled his eyes away, the pleasure was not dimmed.

Slitting his pants with the knife, Amy drew her breath in sharply when she saw how inflamed his wound was. Her face was grave when she said, "I'll have to do something about that, Meade. It can't go any longer."

"Do what you have to do," Meade said and lay back on the blankets.

Amy turned to his pack of supplies and began to sort through them.

Chapter Sixteen

Amy Falcon had little to work with. After building the fire up, she took Childs's gun from the holster and emptied it. The knife proved sharp, and she set it aside, but when she looked for cloth to use as bandages, she found nothing.

Turning away from Meade, Amy slipped out of her shift, then hurriedly put on her damp shirt. Tearing the muslin into strips, she made a careful pile of these on the edge of his blankets.

"Better get something to bite on," she said, and he nodded.

Spreading the slit in his pants, Amy raised the knife and then slit open the festered wound with one clean stroke. The pain hit him like an arrow, and sweat popped out on his forehead and cheeks. Quickly she thrust the barrel of Childs's gun into the fire, and while it grew hot, bathed the festered wound.

He endured more cutting without an outcry, although the leaping shadows on the wall dimmed several times. In a moment she withdrew the .45, the barrel a dull red.

"I'm sorry, Meade," she said, "but this has to be done."

"Do it," he said weakly, and when she pressed the hot barrel against his leg, cried out once and fainted.

The odor of seared flesh made her slightly upset, but she clamped her bottom lip between her teeth and bandaged him well, before hurrying outside.

When she came back in, she pillowed her head in her arms and wept.

Because of his vitality, Meade did not stay out long. He opened his eyes and looked at the ceiling for a moment and could not remember where he was. Amy's soft crying was a low sound, barely audible, and he turned his head slowly to watch her.

Finally he reached out and touched her arm, pulling her until she lay against his chest. Stroking her hair absently, Meade watched the fire dance, a bright cell of light pushing back the dismal day. At last she put her hands against his chest and sat up. Her hair lay in a sodden ruin around her shoulders.

He said, "Why did you come to me, Amy?"

She sat quietly, then murmured, "There wasn't anyone else, Meade." He nodded absently, and she added, "You and June didn't have much time, did you?"

"If you're trying to say something, then say it!"

She stopped the small movements of her hands. "Sorry," she said. "I was prying again, wasn't I?"

"Forget it," he mumbled, the resentment and anger dying quickly. "Let's skip the whole thing, shall we?"

"Whatever you say," she murmured. "You're human, Meade, and I don't blame you for snapping at me, but I think you're mad at yourself. I think you don't love her anymore and she found it out. She must be lonely and confused now. More than you are."

He had no answer and let a silence descend. Throughout the weeping day they remained in the cave, and when darkness was not far off, Meade began to feel restless. He stared at the fire for a moment, then said, "Help me onto my horse, Amy. I'm getting out of here."

Her head came up quickly, and she stared at him. "You can't do that, Meade! You need rest before you can travel."

He struggled to his feet and leaned against the cave wall when dizziness hit him. This passed in a moment, and he said, "With you or without you, Amy, I'm going. I'm tired of running and hiding like a damn animal. I'm going to get Conover the hard way."

"You're a fool, Meade."

"So I'm a fool," he said in a dry voice. "Make up your mind, Amy."

"Of course I'll go with you," she said and went outside to saddle the horses.

Reilly and Sam Sinclair disliked hiding as much as Meade Bigelow. By nature they were restless men, which made their mountain retreat all the more unendurable. Murray was still confined to his bed, but he sat up now, usually with a gun in his lap, for the Sinclairs had a guest.

Garvey was very uncomfortable in the presence of these rough men, for he had been treated sadly when Sam first took him prisoner. Because he was surly and uncooperative, Reilly and Sam had hit him repeatedly until Garvey lost all belligerence. Now he remained quiet, speaking when spoken to, but otherwise, a model guest.

Their cabin sat on a high bench, rimmed on all sides by towering peaks. The remains of an old mine opened up into the hillside a hundred yards away from the cabin entrance. Reilly and Sam walked across the sloping yard and came into the cabin.

Sam said, "I've had a bellyful, Murray. I'm going in."

"That marshal will pick you up," Murray replied, looking from Sam to Reilly. "You going in together?"

"Kind of figured I would," Reilly admitted. "We might stop off at Barnum's place on the way back."

"Be damn careful now," Murray warned. "If you see Hardesty, find out what the hell's happened to Meade."

"I'll do that," Reilly said and nodded to Sam before going outside.

Their horses were picketed in a lean-to in back

of the cabin, and they saddled up. They mounted, swung their horses south, and three hours later they were pounding across the flats behind Jorgenson's place.

Because Reilly was not much for talk and Sam had learned to respect his brother's silence, the ride was a silent one. By noon they left the valley and cut through the slanting rain toward another ridge, reaching the summit an hour later.

Below, Great Northern was like a slumbering beast; no sound came from the mine shaft, and the smelter showed no sign of smoke from the tall stack. Reilly looked at his brother and said, "What the hell?"

"You tell me," Sam said. "Let's go take a look."

"Let's get in to Silver City," Reilly suggested. "I don't want one of those mine guards throwing a slug at me."

Sam shrugged and said no more about it. He turned his horse and angled off the ridge to hit the mine road fifteen minutes later. Out of the rough land now, they increased their pace to a lope and held it until they reached the end of Lode Street.

Reilly stabled the horses but left the saddles on. Together they walked up the street, watching both sides for any sign of the marshal. At the saloon, Reilly wiped his mouth with his hand and said, "Just one, then let's get out of here."

Lonigan was behind the bar washing beer taps down with soda water when Reilly and Sam came in. His mouth opened in surprise, and he said, "Are you two crazy? That damned marshal's liable to came back anytime now!"

"Let's have some whisky," Sam said and turned slightly so he could watch the door. "You say the marshal's gone? Where?"

"I don't know," Lonigan murmured and filled two glasses. "He left town yesterday and hasn't come back yet."

"Jim Hardesty around?"

"The hotel, I guess." Lonigan rested his hands on the edge of the bar and listened. No sounds came from Lode Street. "Dead, ain't it?"

"Where's all the miners?" Reilly asked.

Lonigan's shoulder rose and fell. "Great Northern waitin' for the mine to open. People are gettin' nervous, boys."

The Sinclairs finished their drink and went out. Pausing on the boardwalk, they saw no traffic on the street and they crossed over to the hotel. The lobby was empty; no one was at the desk. Reilly nodded, and Sam followed him up the stairs.

He rapped lightly on Jim Hardesty's door, and a moment later it opened. Hardesty looked up and down the hall quickly and said, "You took a hell of a chance." He closed the door after them, and they took chairs.

"You seen Meade?" Sam asked.

"Yesterday," Hardesty admitted and walked to the window. He stared at the vacant street for a moment, then added, "It's too damned quiet. People are talkin' and wonderin', and that ain't good."

"Lonigan tells me Childs ain't come back yet," Sam said.

"That's right," Hardesty murmured. He slapped the wall with the flat of his hand and spun around. "I'm sure he didn't follow me—positive of it!"

"He's someplace," Reilly murmured and pawed his face out of shape. "I notice Amy Falcon's place is closed up. Where's she?"

"I don't know," Hardesty said, and a great worry was in his eyes. "Dammit, I've been hatin' to think about it. She probably went to him, because she's that way. But she didn't follow me, I'd swear to it. I stayed in the rocks all the way."

Reilly sat hunched over in his chair, idly rotating his hat in his hands. Finally he said, "When it comes to shooting a man I do pretty good, but this is way over my head. If Childs has got Meade Bigelow, the best thing for us to do is hightail it right out of the country."

"Forget that!" Hardesty snapped. "Meade's all right, I tell you."

"You're guessin'," Sam said. "Face it, Jim—you don't know. None of us do. Conover's played us into a big hole, and there ain't a rope long enough to reach us. When the time comes he'll buy the jury that convicts us and pay for the rope that stretches our necks."

"You two stay here," Hardesty said. "I'm goin' to see Fred Allendale."

"He can't help you," Reilly said.

"He knows what makes one dollar stick to another," Hardesty murmured. "Maybe he can outguess Conover."

"You can't outguess the devil," Sam said, and Hardesty went out. Passing through the lobby, he paused on the boardwalk, then walked toward the bank on the far corner.

Curtains were drawn tight over the windows, and the door was locked when he rattled it. He was about to turn away when he heard footfalls inside and Allendale's voice.

"It's Hardesty," he said. "Let me talk to you."

The bolt slid back, and the door opened. From the end of the street, a horse's hoofs made a sodden plop in the muddy street. Allendale paused with the door open while Cord Butram dismounted by the deserted feed store.

He had his coat buttoned, and on the outside, a cartridge belt sagged slightly. A holstered Colt sat on his right hip. "I don't like this," Allendale murmured, and Butram came across the street with high steps. He stamped his feet to remove the mud, and when he looked at Allendale and Hardesty, there was a mild amusement in his eyes.

"Your bank is closed, Allendale. Keep it that way."

"Are you giving the orders for Great Northern now?"

"Yes, I am," Butram murmured.

"Don't give me any," Hardesty murmured and waited for Butram to take offense.

The tall man reached into his pocket and withdrew the marshal's shield, pinning it onto the front of his coat. "Now," he said, "we have law in Silver City."

"That's very interesting," Allendale said dryly. "Now if you'll excuse me." He nudged Hardesty inside and closed the door in Cord Butram's face.

In Allendale's quiet office, they took chairs, and Hardesty said, "I need some advice, Fred. It could be that Meade and Childs have met up." He shifted in the chair and crossed his legs. "I want to know why Dan Conover closed the mine."

"I couldn't tell you," Allendale said flatly. "Jim, there are a number of reasons, but to guess which one would be shooting in the dark."

"Can Conover reopen the mine when he gets ready?"

"Yes," Allendale said. "Providing the books are audited and the business is clear of debts. Wait a minute! I see what you're driving at, Jim. You don't want Conover, through his financial influence, to control the judge to the extent that he selects an auditor who would falsify a report—is that it?"

"I couldn't have said it like that," Hardesty

admitted, "but that's the general idea. Let's go have a talk with Dan."

Allendale thought about it for a moment, then rose to get his hat and coat. He locked the front door behind him, and together they walked down the street.

The day was gray with intermittent rains, and there was no heat in the sun, for the clouds closed it off, allowing only a milky light to filter through. The tops of the surrounding mountains were blotted out as though erased with a stroke of dull-gray paint.

They traveled along the back street and turned in at Dan Conover's house. Hattie admitted them, ushering them into the study.

Conover seemed in a gay mood, and he puffed his cigar with the air of a thoroughly contented man. He waved them into chairs and passed the cigar box around. He called to Hattie and had drinks served. For thirty minutes, he was the perfect host, then he said, "You gentlemen look worried."

"You know damn well we're worried," Allendale said. "You've gone too far, Dan—closing up everything this way."

Conover laughed, and his cigar tilted sharply between his teeth. "Gentlemen, I have never enjoyed a small victory. I am, in a sense, like the trick shot who dreams of a chance to bounce his bullet off the bear's skull, hit a hawk on the wing, then have the bird fall on a squirrel and break his neck. That is exactly what I've done."

"Make it plain," Hardesty said sourly. "I'm a stupid man."

Taking a place behind his desk, Conover began to tabulate his victories. "The Meade Bigelow-Murray Sinclair clique is intolerable, simply because they would undermine the entire cartel system to the point of collapse. As it stands, my grasp on the corporation is such that I manage, rather than own outright. But by closing down, I can panic the local shareholders, buy them out for a song, and reopen under an entirely new organization. Surely, Allendale, as a businessman you can understand that I have violated no laws but acted in accordance with sound business judgment."

"Someone ought to put a bullet in you," Hardesty said.

Conover raised his hand. "Bigelow has a murder charge over his head now because he believed in violence. Your friends the Sinclairs are wanted for robbery and murder." He paused to snuff out his cigar. "The merchants of Silver City are on the verge of a panic, and I have no intention of stopping it. I don't believe I could if I was inclined to."

Hardesty got up and walked around the room for a moment. "Dan," he said, "a man has to admire a great gambler, and I admire you.

But you're takin' an awful chance. Bigelow is different than most men. If Childs don't catch him, he'll come after you, and when he does, all the law on your side won't help you because he'll blow your damned brains out."

A quick silence came into the room, and Conover sat motionless. Finally he laughed uneasily. "No man is that much of a fool," he said. "Meade is under arrest at this moment. My daughter followed you yesterday, Hardesty, and I am told that Childs followed her. I know she saw Meade Bigelow. She did not even speak to me when she came home soaking wet from the rain."

"You sly son of a bitch," Hardesty murmured.

"I will take that as a compliment," Conover said and found a ready smile. "Now if you gentlemen will excuse me." He got up and opened the door for them. "You're licked—admit it. The idea won't seem so bad once you get used to it."

Once out of the house, Allendale let his mask slip and he was a defeated man. "Now," he said, "I can understand why financiers blow their brains out and jump out of windows."

"He can't get away with a swindle like this!" Hardesty said.

"But he can," Allendale murmured. "Bankers do it every day on a smaller scale." He put his hand on Hardesty's shoulder as they walked along. "The essence of business is to pass a dollar from hand to hand and get a little of it to stick to you. As a banker, I've loaned money to a man and taken a mortgage on his land or home, knowing full well when I loaned him the money that he couldn't pay it off. Perhaps he put five hundred dollars into it; that was profit for me. And I had the land, or the bank had it, whichever way you prefer to think of it. Over a period of years, I might acquire a lot of property, and if all went well, stand to realize a fortune from it, providing my judgment was sound."

"He was lying when he said Childs caught Meade!"

"Don't be too sure," Allendale said. "Meade couldn't hide forever, and Childs is like a bulldog. I think he was a little ahead of himself, but Childs was on Meade's trail."

They turned the corner of Lode and stopped. People stood along the boardwalks, and on the other corner, a large group waited before Allendale's bank.

"I think it's started," Allendale murmured and moved forward.

Several men saw them approaching and left the group, and by the time they were halfway there, the mob was around them, moving with them, all shouting to be heard first.

When Allendale reached the bank, he stopped, his back to the door. Jim Hardesty stood beside him, his hand hooked in his shell belt. Waving his hands, Allendale brought quiet to the crowd, then said, "You're exciting yourselves for nothing. There is nothing I can do."

"I got three hundred dollars in there!" one man shouted. "By God, I want it now!"

"The bank is closed," Allendale said. "No money goes in or out until Great Northern is cleared through auditing."

The crowd began to raise their voices again until a din rose along the street. Several men walking along the boardwalks paused to try the doors of the various stores, but they were all locked.

One man stopped before the mercantile, looked in the window for a moment, then took his gun and smashed the large window. He reached in, took a blanket, and threw it around his shoulders and walked down the street.

The crowd confronting Allendale and Hardesty was getting ugly, and Hardesty murmured, "Open the door, Fred. I'll cover you."

Allendale produced his key, and the crowd began to yell louder, but Hardesty dropped his hand to his gun in the swivel holster and tipped the muzzle up. This held them while Allendale opened the door, and then Hardesty ducked inside.

Almost immediately they began to batter at the door, and one of the front windows broke in a shower of glass. Hardesty shot into the frame and heard a man's answering yelp of surprise. He said, "We can't hold 'em, Fred. They'll wreck the place."

Looking around a room that represented twenty years of building, Allendale said softly, "Only the furniture." He turned and went to the back door with Hardesty following him, while at the front of the building, men began battering at the stout panel with a ram.

In the alley, Allendale paused and mopped his perspiring brow. "They're going crazy," he said and listened to windows being broken along Lode Street. The town was no longer quiet for men were caught up in the mood to plunder, and they took what they wanted, smashing anything that barred their way.

"We can go up the back way to the hotel," Hardesty said and moved down the alley. Night was not far off, and the remaining daylight was murky and cheerless. They went up the back steps of the hotel, entered the upper hall, and went into Hardesty's room.

Reilly and Sam Sinclair had pulled chairs up to the window to watch the rioting crowd below. Allendale sat on the edge of Hardesty's bed, showing no inclination to watch.

Reilly said, "Sam and I could go down there in another thirty minutes, and with the dark, no one would recognize us."

"Better stay put," Hardesty murmured. "I think Childs has got Meade."

"Son of a bitch," Sam murmured. He pointed to a man standing by Karen's Saloon, watching the milling men pull the town apart. "Ain't that Cord Butram? He's wearin' a damn badge."

"New town marshal," Hardesty said. "Stay away from him. He's rougher than he looks."

"That's what I'm going to find out," Reilly said. "I've taken enough of this crap." He put on his hat and moved toward the door. "Comin', Sam?"

"I guess I will at that," Sam said and left with him.

Chapter Seventeen

Reilly and Sam Sinclair passed through the lobby, then paused on the hotel porch to watch the men rioting in the street. There was no purpose in the destruction, for they were destroying the thing they wished to save.

"Like a pack of wolves turned loose," Sam murmured. "Like a bunch of kids, all right until someone breaks a window and gets away with it. Then they'll stand there and break 'em all."

Cord Butram was still standing by the saloon, and Reilly pulled on Sam's sleeve. They both left the porch and began to battle their way up the street. There was not much light left, and no lamps had been lighted to push back the growing night. Three doors up from the hotel, Reilly left the boardwalk and crossed the muddy street.

Moving along easily, they approached the saloon from a flat angle and were fifteen feet from the porch when Cord Butram saw them. He took his cigar from his mouth and threw it into the street.

"This is a catch," Butram said and shifted slightly, facing them squarely.

"You haven't caught us," Sam murmured, and a smile lifted the ends of his lips. He nodded toward the men in the street. "You like to watch the town go boom?"

"Let them wreck it," he said. "Right now I'm interested in you. Drop your gunbelts and surrender to proper authority!"

"You're not the law," Sam said. "Maybe Great Northern law, but to me you're just a crumb. Get out of the way, Cord. We want a drink."

"I think you'll have to move me," Butram said.

"That can be arranged," Sam said. "But I'll do it the permanent way."

Butram laughed. "Sam, I've stood by for three years and watched you thumb your nose at Great Northern. I've always wanted to teach you better manners."

Without warning he drew and fired, and the bullet sent Sam stumbling back until he fell off the boardwalk and into the muddy street. Reilly drew his gun as Butram cocked for the second shot, catching the tall man in the pit of the stomach as Butram triggered again.

Butram sagged against the wall of the saloon and tried to lift his heavy gun, but the weight suddenly pulled his arm down, and he rolled off the porch.

The sudden blast of gunfire drew a blanket of quiet over the men in the street, and they stared as Butram tried to get up, then fell back unmoving. Reilly holstered his gun and lifted his brother, but Sam was dead.

Darkness was deeper in the street now, and men

255

were but shadowy shapes that moved restlessly. Lifting his brother, Reilly staggered a little under Sam's weight and made his way down the street to the stable.

Hardesty came out of the hotel and left the porch in a rush, bowling one man over in his haste to follow Reilly Sinclair. He shoved men aside and hurried to the stable.

Reilly had lit a lantern and hung it in the arch where it puddled light onto the straw-littered floor. Sam was draped across the saddle, and Reilly straightened as Hardesty came in.

The ex-marshal looked at Sam's lax face and said, "Some things turn out like hell, no matter how you look at it." The sound of horses plodding along the muddy road drew his attention, and he moved behind a corner post, searching the darkness intently.

He stifled an oath and moved forward as Meade Bigelow and Amy Falcon came under the circle of light and stopped. Meade slid from his horse and hobbled when he walked. Amy dismounted and put her arm around him to support him as Hardesty and Reilly came forward.

"Jesus," Reilly said. "We thought Childs had you, Meade."

"He did have me," Meade said and turned his head toward the town. "Sounds like they're breaking it up."

"They've gone crazy," Hardesty said. "Conover's driven them into a panic. He'll own it all when this is over."

"Maybe he'll be dead when this is over," Meade said softly and looked at Hardesty. "Go home, Amy. Go home and stay there."

"No," she said. "You're going to do something foolish and stupid, I know the signs now."

"I said, go home," Meade repeated. He disengaged her arm from around his waist and gave her a shove. "Take the back streets and you'll be safe."

"You better go," Hardesty murmured and waited.

She looked at Meade steadily, then raised her hand in a pleading gesture. Dropping it, she whirled and ran. The night covered her immediately.

"Cord Butram is dead," Reilly said. "I killed him, Meade, after he shot Sam."

In Meade's eyes something bleak appeared, and his face turned grave. "Sorry, Reilly, but I think you had the right idea. The time for deals and talk is over now. From here on in, we do it with a gun."

"Where's Childs?" Hardesty asked. "Meade, you didn't—?"

"He was walking the last I saw of him," Meade said and listened to the yelling along Lode Street. "Seems like a good time to do a little busting of our own, don't it?"

He had difficulty walking for he had to keep

his leg stiff. Pain made sweat pop out on his forehead, but he crossed the street, with Hardesty and Reilly bringing up the rear.

At the darkened doorway of the Silver City Land and Trust Company, Meade drew Childs's gun and shot the lock away. They went in and Meade said, "Prop something against that door. I don't want to be interrupted."

Going into Dan Conover's office, Meade touched a match to several lamps and closed the inner door. He sat down at the large desk with a stack of ledgers and began to go through them patiently, making many notations on a piece of paper.

An hour dragged by, then two, and Reilly exhibited signs of strain. "How long you going to keep at this?" he asked.

"Until I get some answers," Meade murmured and worked on.

At eleven, he rummaged through one of the drawers until he found a box of cigars. After smoking three in a row, he pushed the stack of ledgers away from him and said, "I think I'm going to kill a man."

Hardesty's breathing was loud in the room. Outside, the street had quieted some, but still men moved up and down, shouting and smashing any stray window left intact. "What did you find out, Meade?" Hardesty asked.

"Conover's other set of books," Meade said

and stared at the wall. "This is the real thing, Jim. All the money actually made from all these enterprises is here, intact, but the dividends were paid on the set of books Cord Butram kept at the mine."

"June kept books for her father," Hardesty said.

"Yes," Meade said. "She knew that he was a swindler."

"Sorry," Hardesty murmured and dropped his eyes.

"Now I know where the money goes," Meade said. "To banks in St. Paul and Detroit and Kansas City—safety-deposit boxes that belong to Dan Conover." Meade slapped the desk. "That Metropolitan Trust Company in Baltimore—I'll bet it's a listing and nothing more. Those shares mean money invested, but where did he get that money? Who's behind him, Jim?"

"Hell," Hardesty said, "I don't know."

"I think you do," Meade said. "I think you know and don't realize it. What kind of tie do you have to Conover, Jim? Something in his past, maybe?"

"No," Hardesty said and cocked his head to one side. "I had a reputation and he contacted me, offered me a good salary, and I took him up on it. That's all, Meade."

"Allene knew him," Reilly murmured and glanced quickly at Hardesty. "Sorry, Jim, but Jean overheard her talking to Heavy Pearl."

Meade sat motionless for a full minute. "Is that so, Jim?"

"Yeah," Hardesty said softly. "Meade, you can see why I didn't say anything. Allene's all right. I don't want her smeared with anything, you understand."

"She's not going to be," Meade said and stood up clumsily. "Snuff out the lamps, Reilly." He shuffled to the door and when the room was dark, moved the barricade aside from the door and stepped out.

Darkness lay thick and unbroken along the street while a few men from the mines paraded up and down with lanterns lashed to poles. The bobbing light made eerie splashes, and Meade edged along the building wall, moving slowly to favor his leg.

At the corner, Meade crossed Lode, with Hardesty and Reilly tagging along. On the back street he found Heavy Pearl's house and mounted the porch. The door was locked, and Hardesty said, "Let me," and broke it down with two lunges of his shoulder.

The two girls were in the parlor, and Jean cried out with relief when she saw Reilly. He went to her and began to talk softly. From the back of the house, Heavy Pearl's slippers whispered on the floor, and she gasped when she saw Meade Bigelow standing in the middle of her parlor.

"Let's have a little talk, Pearl," Meade said and

placed a hand flat against her chest, shoving her deeper into the hall. She put up a mild battle, then suddenly quit and parted the bead drapes.

"Look around," Meade said, and Hardesty opened drawers and snooped in the closet. Pearl sat down in a heavy chair and watched for a moment. When she grew nervous, Meade sat down across from her and said, "Let's have a talk, Pearl. An honest one."

"What about?"

"Money," Meade said, "and Great Northern."

"The only money I see is two dollars at a whack, and I run a house, not Great Northern."

"All right," Meade said pleasantly. "Let's talk about Dan Conover."

"I only know him when we meet on the street," Pearl said. "What the hell are you driving at?"

"I think you know him real well," Meade murmured. "Tell me how you met in Kansas City, Pearl?"

"Who says I knew him there?"

"Allene says so."

"She lies," Pearl murmured. "You're barking up the wrong tree."

"Hey, Meade," Hardesty said quickly. "Who do these belong to?" He threw a pair of slippers onto the floor, and from behind Pearl's dresses he withdrew three suits, a half dozen shirts, and a man's flowered dressing gown. "Just Conover's size," Hardesty said and stopped searching.

Meade leaned forward. "Well, Pearl?"

She moved her shoulders in a shrug. "They could belong to a hundred different men."

"But they don't," Meade said flatly. "You've been in the business a long time. Do you invest your money, Pearl? Stocks, bonds, or did you put it in Dan Conover?"

"What are you trying to prove?" Pearl snapped. "Get out of here and leave me alone."

"Not yet," Meade said, and his face held no compassion for her. "I can figure it out, Pearl. I'll spread it around just the way I figure it, right or wrong."

"No! You wouldn't do that, Meade. You're a fair man. I've never heard of you hitting below the belt."

"Now I am," he said flatly. "Pearl, Dan Conover is a dead man, only he don't know it yet."

"No!" She shouted this. "All right, Meade. I'll give it to you straight. I knew him in Kansas City. He was a restless man, full of energy. He and his wife—well, she never did him any good, and Dan was a man who couldn't wait, you understand. He came to me, and we sort of fell together. I could offer him something without him feeling obligated afterward—you know how that is, don't you? No, I guess you wouldn't.

"I was younger then and prettier. He had some money so he loaned it to me, and I started a place of my own. Times were booming then, and money came easy. I was kind of saving, but then Dan got into that tight one back there and moved on.

"A while later he sent for me, and I opened up another place. We sort of drifted together after that, steady, you understand. His wife found out that he was seeing a woman and ran away. I guess you know about that. After that we spent a lot of time together."

"About the money," Meade prodded. "Pearl, where did he get the money to dummy up these companies on paper and back them himself?"

"Sure I gave it to him," she said. "Why shouldn't I have given it to him? We loved each other. We were partners right down the line."

Meade shook his head slowly. "Pearl, I just looked over the Trust Company's books, and you've been took. He's made the big steal, Pearl, the easy money. Over a million dollars' worth."

"You're lying," she snapped. "He might have stole and juggled the books from the other suckers, but not from me."

"He got you, too," Meade murmured and felt slightly sorry for her. She had so little to offer a man, and the insecurity of her position was tragic, for she had no way to fight back. "On paper, the bank deposits in St. Paul are controlled by the Trust Company in Baltimore. The same is true of the bank deposits in Kansas City and Detroit. Everything is under the Metropolitan

Trust of Baltimore, Pearl. You'll never touch a nickel of that money, because only Dan Conover can get it. He's chairman of the 'board' of the Trust Company back East."

She sat with her mouth open, speechless. Finally she said, "He wouldn't do that to me. No, he wouldn't!"

"He has and he meant to," Meade said flatly. "Pearl, a man can climb so high that he can't see the dirty bottom where he started. Dan's done that, and you're on the outside looking in. Whatever you invested is lost now, Pearl. Whatever he managed to corner is his and not yours. He's finished with you, just like he's finished with Silver City. Dan Conover burns what he doesn't want, never leaves it for someone else."

Heavy Pearl's face began to break, and tears formed on the bottom eyelids. The heavy lip rouge she wore seemed to make her look much older, and lines appeared around her lips and eyes.

This was something Meade didn't want to look at, and he stood up carefully, favoring his leg. He glanced at Hardesty and shook his head, then looked around as the bead drapes stirred.

Reilly looked sick, and then Meade saw Homer Childs behind him.

Childs said, "Please, Bigelow. Don't make me shoot you."

He gave Reilly a shove that sent him into the

room and then covered all of them with his gun. His clothes were muddy and rain had ruined his hat, but his eyes were alive and pleased. Fatigue etched deep lines on his forehead, but the gun was steady.

"We come to the end now, don't we?" He smiled faintly. "That was a long walk to Barnum's place. He was good enough to let me have a horse, although I had to threaten him with arrest first."

Reilly seemed deeply ashamed. "He came in suddenly, Meade, and had the drop on me before I could do anything."

"It's all right," Meade said and shifted his feet. "I'm ready to go, Childs. I think I'm as tired of dodging you as you are of chasing me."

"That's fine," Childs said and stepped back so Meade could move past him. Dragging his leg, Meade stumbled and caught at the drapes, but whirled then and clubbed down on Childs's gun arm.

The long-barreled Smith & Wesson clattered on the floor, and Reilly dived for it, covering it with his body. Childs hit Meade a driving blow, but Hardesty moved in quickly, locking his arm around Childs's neck and shutting off the marshal's wind.

"Don't hurt him," Meade said quickly, and Hardesty released him, shoving him into a chair. Hardesty tipped up his holster and centered the muzzle on Childs's chest.

"Be good now," Hardesty said and looked at Meade who was getting painfully to his feet. Reilly tucked the marshal's gun in his waistband and waited.

"Let me have paper and pencil," Meade murmured and Heavy Pearl found some in a battered writing desk. For ten minutes Meade wrote, the scratch of the pencil sharp in the stillness. Finally he folded it and gave it to Reilly.

"Take this to Jerry, the telegrapher at the mine. Put a gun on him if you have to, but see that it gets out. Have them send it back to make sure it got through all right. This is important!"

"He'll send it with his damn feet if he has to," Reilly said and ducked out.

"Now," Meade said and pulled in a gusty breath. "We got a little pressing business. Bring Childs with us, Jim, and see that he behaves himself."

"He'll behave," Hardesty promised and nodded toward the hall as Meade went out. Together they left the house, crossed Lode Street, and made their way down the darkened back street toward Dan Conover's house.

Chapter Eighteen

When Meade stopped on the corner of the back street, Childs said, "Listen to me, Bigelow. You wouldn't shoot a federal officer."

"That's right," Meade agreed, "but you try anything and I'll break your skull with a gun barrel."

Childs fell silent and moved on when Hardesty prodded him with his gun. Every home sported lamplight in the windows while the citizens of Silver City sought safety within their four walls.

Meade had to move slowly because of his leg, and he crossed the street when they came abreast of Conover's house. Mounting the porch, Meade did not bother to knock, just opened the door and let himself in.

"Keep your mouth shut, Childs," Hardesty warned softly, and in the parlor, June turned her head quickly at this slight sound. She saw Meade and left her chair with a rush. When she tried to put her arms around him, he pushed her aside.

"So you didn't know who the money went to?"

She turned pale and then said, "Meade, did you want me to betray my own father?"

"I wanted you to be honest," he murmured. "He in the study?" She said nothing, and he brushed past her to open the study door. Conover was behind his desk in his padded chair, and he looked up quickly at this intrusion.

"Look out!" June screamed, and Conover jerked open a desk drawer, but froze when he saw Meade's gun.

"Keep your hands in sight," Meade advised, and Hardesty pushed Childs into the room. "Sit down, Childs," Meade said, and the marshal lowered himself without protest.

"Get out of my house!" Conover thundered, but Meade just smiled and sat on the corner of the desk, his gun resting on his thigh.

Hardesty closed the door, and June wrung her hands, silently pleading with Meade, but he wouldn't look at her. Conover's nerve began to break, and sweat appeared on his face.

"So you finally cornered it?" Meade said. "Dan, I have to hand it to you. You're a real, top-drawer crook."

"I can forgive that," Conover said. "A murderer's statement is of little value."

"Maybe you won't be able to pin murder on me," Meade said. "Cord Butram is dead, and Garvey has changed his tune. He's ready to swear that I shot Garroway in self-defense." Meade smiled as Conover went white-faced. "Rocks you, doesn't it? I'll tell you something else, Dan. Heavy Pearl knows now that you've swindled her. The secret's out about you and her."

"You lying swine!" Conover said, flicking

his eyes to his daughter. "You don't believe his lies, do you? I love your mother, and I've been faithful to her. He's trying to set you against me so he can have you for himself!"

Meade shook his head. "You're wasting your breath, Dan. It's all over but the shouting and building back what you've torn down."

"Bigelow," Childs said, "I give you fair warning now. Carry this any farther and I'll see that you hang."

"You're not going to hang me," Meade said softly. "You want to hang somebody, hang Dan Conover for what he's done to this country."

Some of Conover's confidence returned, and he touched a match to a fresh cigar, completely controlled now. "Meade," he said, "I find this rather amusing now that the shock of your entry has passed. You say that I have been a chaser and a business partner of Heavy Pearl." He chuckled. "I think you would find that difficult to prove, my boy." He shook his finger at Meade. "You'll not find one scrap of paper that will link her name with mine.

"No," he added. "You've been out-trumped, Meade. Face it. Surrender to the law and stand trial for your deed."

"What about all those people out on the street?" Childs asked softly. "I heard that closing down the mine will ruin them."

"Perhaps that is so," Conover said firmly, "but

a man can't do business and watch out for the other fellow all the time. In a rough game, people get hurt. It's unfortunate, but it happens."

"I looked over your books," Meade said. "You got quite a little nest egg put away, haven't you?"

Conover pointed his cigar like a gun barrel. "And every bit of it perfectly legal! You'll find no flies on me, Meade. You're whipped and you'd better admit it."

"You're shrewd," Meade admitted. "Now all you'll have to do is take a little business trip back East, pick up your accounts, and then sit back and laugh at us because we've been a bunch of fools."

"That," Conover snapped, "is legal also, or so you will soon find out."

"Two sets of books," Meade murmured. "How can you get out of that one, Dan? When the auditing is over, a federal warrant will be out for you."

"You're mistaken," Conover said and could not hold back his smile. "When the audit is over, you will find that my share of the profits, with my name on the checks, has been taken from the Great Northern books the same as each of you. If you've been short-changed, then so have I."

"Wait a minute," Childs said, sitting upright in his chair. "You're admitting to a discrepancy in the bookkeeping?"

"Why not?" Conover murmured. "What can

be proved against me?" He laughed and flicked ashes from his cigar. "I admit nothing here, and Meade's accusations will not stand up in court. My shirt tail is clean, gentlemen. I defy you to make anything different out of it."

"Sure," Meade told Childs. "Now all he'll have to do is to go back East and pick up that million dollars he's got stashed." He turned to Conover. "I think I got you where the hair is short, Dan. Just before we came over here, I sent a telegram back East, and by morning, there'll be a court order out to open those accounts and have them dispersed as legal profits."

Conover seemed about to have a stroke. His cigar fell to the floor and lay there, and he stood slack-jawed, both hands gripping the edge of his desk.

"You're broke," Meade told him. "Stone-broke. The mine is shut down, and you can't open it. When the books are audited now the smell of fraud will be so bad even you won't be able to stand it. The million dollars is gone, Dan— *pppfffttt!* You haven't got the price of a good cigar!"

When Conover tried to speak, no words came out, and it seemed that he was about to strangle. "Murray did have the silver that you ordered looted from your own company," Meade added. "It's safe at Marilee Hart's logging camp."

Childs began to get interested. "Are you saying

271

that the Sinclairs aren't guilty of robbery and murder?"

"No more than I am," Meade said and turned his attention back to Dan Conover. "I'll do something for you, and I hope it's the last human kindness you ever receive. Take your hat and walk out of here. Heavy Pearl's stuck by you all these years, and she'll probably be fool enough to go with you. Get out, Dan. I'm giving you your life and a running start."

"You can't do that," Childs said flatly. "He will have to submit to arrest."

"Then go catch him," Meade snapped. "You had to with me."

Hardesty prodded the old man. "You'd better go, Dan. It's the best thing."

"All right," Conover mumbled and picked up his hat. He moved to the door and stopped by his daughter's elbow. "Do you hate me, honey?"

"I don't know," she said. "If I do it's not for what you've done here, but what you've done to Mother."

Conover seemed at a loss for words. He made aimless motions with his hands, then said, "You have to understand how it is with a man. Take good care of your mother."

"Good-by," she said coldly and turned away from him. Conover waited a moment longer, then went out and down the darkened street.

June stood with her face to the paneled wall, and Hardesty shifted his feet nervously.

He said, "Do I need this anymore?" He wiggled the muzzle of his gun, and Childs shook his head.

Sighing, he stood up and said, "The real work and worry is just beginning, Bigelow. The town will go crazy, and everyone will be grabbing for what they can hang on to."

"What about the charges against Murray and me?" Meade asked.

"It'll take some time," he murmured, "but I imagine you'll still be here if we need you for anything?"

He glanced at June Conover and moved toward the door. Hardesty looked at Meade, then at the girl, and followed him. Childs looked as though he had something else to say, but let it go.

The door slammed, and a deep silence came into the room.

Meade leaned against the back of a chair to ease his leg. "What can a man say?" he murmured. "I had to break him, June. I had to break him hard."

"Does it make any difference?" She turned around and met his eyes. "You fought as dirty a fight as he did. Did you have to say that about Heavy Pearl?"

"When you wipe a thing clean, then do it well," Meade said. He continued to watch her for many moments, trying to read her thoughts, to gain a clue to her feelings, but he could discover nothing.

"You want out, don't you?" Her voice was even and without care one way or another.

"I didn't say it."

"You don't have to," June said. "We made a mistake, you and I. I knew it right away."

For a moment he had no words to answer her. "Tomorrow you may feel different."

"I won't feel different then," she said with a positiveness that he didn't miss. "We're not alike, Meade. We'll never be alike, and we might as well understand it. When I kept those books, I never thought of my father as a crook, just a smart man who used his brains to get ahead. Up in the rocks, I was having fun because I wanted to, but it worried you. We're not the same, Meade. There's too much of my mother in me in some ways, and too much of my father in the other."

"That's being honest about it anyway," he said.

"Sometimes I can be like you," she murmured and turned away from him. "Leave me alone now, Meade. We don't owe each other a damn thing."

"All right," he said and limped toward the door.

Her voice halted him, and he turned to look at her. "I'm not hurting you, am I, Meade? I don't think you really love me, because I'm not what you want in a woman." She smiled faintly.

"I don't think I would ever have gone out in a rainstorm after you."

In Meade's mind, that summed up the difference. June could never give herself to anyone, while Amy Falcon had spent a lifetime doing just that. When he understood this, opening the door was easy, and he didn't look back as he went out and slowly down the dark path.

The town was still alive, but there was some organization to the sound now, a different tempo. Hardesty was out there with Childs, handling the crowd, moving them into some semblance of order.

Meade listened awhile, then turned down the lane, walking carefully lest he fall and be unable to get up. There was a light in Amy Falcon's cabin, and he rapped on the door, lightly, and listened for the whisper of her slippers on the bare floor.

"Who is it?" she asked through the door.

"Meade." The bolt slid back, and he stepped inside.

Her hair was wet from her bath, and her robe clung tightly to her. "Coffee?" she said.

"It would go fine about now," he murmured and hobbled to the table.

"You ought to be off of that," she said and slid his cup and saucer on the drainboard of the sink. She poured and handed him the cup. "You beat him, didn't you?"

"Yes."

"Is he still alive?"

"Running," Meade murmured. "I've finished him here, with his family—I did it and I'm not proud of it."

"All fights," she said, "can be dirty when the stakes are high enough. What will happen now, Meade? A wide-open town?"

He sipped the scalding brew. "More or less. Childs and Hardesty are holding it together. It will be a month or more before the legal work and auditing is over. There'll be a disbursement of Conover's bank accounts. I think it'll help restore things to an even keel. After that it'll be every man for himself."

She sat on the edge of the table, her long legs outstretched and rounded beneath her robe. "Will Hardesty stay?" Meade nodded. "He'll have to watch her, won't he? I guess he loves her and wants it that way." She shrugged. "Sometimes it's hard to say what people want, isn't it, Meade?"

"Go ahead and ask it," he said.

Now that she was facing the question, she did not want to put it into words. Finally she said, "Are you going to marry her now?"

"No," he said. "She let me off the hook, because she had to. I'm glad it was that way, Amy. I'd hurt her enough. It was her turn to hit back, and if it didn't hurt too much, I don't think any harm was done by pretending otherwise."

She nodded and murmured, "Jim Hardesty has a lot about Allene to forget, hasn't he? Can he really do that, Meade? Can he wipe it all out as though none of it ever happened?"

"He already has," Meade said and finished his cup. He meant to move away from the table, but she took the cup away from him and took it to the sink. After she rinsed it, she stood with her back to him, her hands braced along the edge.

"Why did you come here, Meade? Why do you always keep coming back?"

"You keep calling me back," he said. "There have been times when I told myself that I wouldn't come back anymore, but I always do."

"She had what you wanted, class and brains." The intense feeling in Amy's voice caused him to lift his eyes quickly. "Wasn't that enough?"

"It was nothing," he said. "A foolish mistake in judgment that I will always regret." He waited a moment, then added, "Turn around, Amy. Don't hide your face from me."

"Is that what I'm doing?" Her voice was faintly hostile, then she turned to face him. "Sorry, Meade. I never did have the right to snap at you, but I always did."

"No one has a better right," Meade murmured. "That's what I'm trying to tell you, Amy. You always were the one, only I couldn't see it."

She watched him steadily, and for a moment he thought she had ceased to breathe. He added, "I guess I've bungled this, too, waiting too long. I guess it would be hard for you to forget—I treated you pretty badly, but I'm a steady man, Amy."

"Meade," she said tenderly and moved away from the sink. "Shut up, Meade." She paused near the table, her right side toward him. "I wouldn't play games with you, Meade, because I've loved you for a long time. With me it's all or nothing at all."

"I don't smell of Bay Rum," he said and smiled. "And I forgot the flowers, but as for the other—" He reached out and grabbed her by the arm, pulling her off balance and against him.

She pushed against him with both hands, not frightened or surprised, but stubbornly determined. Meade laughed softly and fastened a hand in her long hair and pulled her head back. She squirmed when he pressed his lips against hers, then her struggling stopped and she hugged him tightly.

For a time they stood there, and then he released her but she didn't move away. Her lips turned up in a smile, and the lamp glistened in a thousand gleams in her eyes. She said, "I don't think I'll ever give another thought to you and June Conover."

He held her close, and then she bent over and cupped her hand around the lamp chimney and brought a deep darkness into the room with a quick puff.

The sounds of the town were dead now, and a deep quiet lay over the land. He felt her stir against him, and her lips brushed his cheek. The dawn was not far away and he was eager for it, for when it came, a new life would begin.

He kissed her again, then put all thoughts of tomorrow out of his mind. There was plenty of time. He felt positive of it. . . .

Center Point Large Print
600 Brooks Road / PO Box 1
Thorndike, ME 04986-0001 USA

(207) 568-3717

US & Canada:
1 800 929-9108
www.centerpointlargeprint.com